Halle Butler is the author of *Jillian* and *The New Me*. She has been named a National Book Award Foundation "5 Under 35" honouree and a *Granta* Best Young American Novelist.

Jillian

Halle Butler

WEIDENFELD & NICOLSON

First published in the United States in 2015 by Curbside Splendor
First published in Great Britain in 2020 by Weidenfeld & Nicolson
an imprint of The Orion Publishing Group Ltd
Carmelite House, 50 Victoria Embankment
London EC4Y 0DZ

An Hachette UK Company

1 3 5 7 9 10 8 6 4 2

Chapter 3 originally appeared, in slightly different form, in
The Nervous Breakdown in 2015 and chapter 5 originally appeared, in
slightly different form, in *Hobart* in 2013.

A CIP catalogue record for this book is
available from the British Library.

ISBN (Mass Market Paperback) 978 1 4746 1757 4
ISBN (eBook) 978 1 4746 1758 1

Printed in Great Britain by Clays Ltd, Elcograf S.p.A.

Text designed by Sabrina Bowers

www.orionbooks.co.uk
www.weidenfeldandnicolson.co.uk

Jillian

PART 1

PART 1

Jillian was in the rapture of one of her great musings.

"But what I really want is to be a personal assistant, or to go door-to-door and help people get organized. Not, like, as a psychologist, but I might be good at that, too. More like helping people get the right bins and sort through their stuff. Just go in and help people get organized."

"You really like organizing?" Megan asked. Megan was not listening. She pronounced it flatly. "You really like organizing."

"I'm obsessed," said Jillian. "My house is packed with color-coded boxes and labels and stuff like that."

"You're a collector," said Megan.

Jillian burped, a discreet, air-valve release through her mouth. "Ha ha, yeah."

The phone rang. Megan picked it up and said, "Good afternoon, doctors' office." The woman on the phone asked if this was Dr. Billings's office. Megan answered in the affirmative.

"Well, finally," said the woman. "I left a message on your machine and I did not receive a call within twenty-four hours, as promised."

"How may I help you?" asked Megan.

"I was beginning to think Dr. Billings was a figment of my mind," said the woman. "Like I was imagining him, and that maybe I had dreamed leaving the message."

Megan sniffed.

"But when I checked my call history just now, I saw that I had really called." Megan didn't have the energy.

"Umm, hello, hello," said the woman.

"Yes, how may I help you?" said Megan.

"I'd like to make an appointment, like I said in my message. Should I just start from the top?"

"Could I have your name and availability, please?" said Megan. She thought of her current mindset as "allowing the shit to happen."

The microwave beeped in the background. The microwave was in the closet where they kept drug samples, and it sat on top of the mini-fridge. People used the mini-fridge to store both lunches and biological samples, side by side. Megan did not like to use the mini-fridge or the microwave. She did not like to think about how the heat from the microwave might combine the side-by-side contents of the mini-fridge.

She thought about the microwave and the mini-fridge while scheduling the appointment, and she also thought about how people affectionately referred to using the microwave as "nuking."

"All right, Mrs. Davies, we'll see you next Wednesday at ten o'clock," said Megan.

Jillian walked back to her desk from the microwave, holding her lunch. The lunch came in a small plastic tub and had an indeterminate odor.

Jillian's desk was large—executive, almost—and made of mahogany-colored laminate. Megan's desk was small and made of glass and cheap, black metal, and Megan had decorated the glass with a fanciful pattern of coffee splatters, adhesive, and various other dribblings. Megan's desk was placed in the corner between a fax machine and an oversized, locked trash can. She had a nice view of the wall.

"I mean, don't get me wrong," said Jillian, "I love my job." She peeled the plastic flap off her lunch and slapped it on her desk with a practiced gesture. "But it's a dream of mine to work on my own terms. And I think, you know, when a person has a passion, they should follow it."

"Mmmm," said Megan.

"And since I keep collecting all this organizing stuff, I think it's pretty clear that it's a passion, so I'm trying to really listen to it so I can understand what it means for my future."

Megan squeezed the bridge of her nose.

"I'm sorry?" said Jillian.

"Oh, nothing, I'm sorry. I was talking to my computer."

"Oh, don't worry. I do that all the time," said Jillian. She laughed. "So what do you think of my idea? Do you think about that stuff sometimes?"

"Yeah, I guess. I don't know about organizers, though,"

said Megan. She dropped her voice an octave for the authoritative thrill. "I think sometimes people buy organizers to make themselves feel satisfied with their intentions, rather than to help them organize."

"Hmmm, that's interesting," said Jillian.

"It's just an opinion."

"It's cool how different people are," said Jillian.

"Yeah, maybe," said Megan.

"So, Miss Megan, what's your dream job? Go ahead and describe it to me."

Jillian was a thirty-five-year-old woman. Megan was twenty-four.

"Gee, I don't know," said Megan. She looked around the office. "I guess this." She widened her eyes at her keyboard. "I guess I would like to have a job that's easy like this, but maybe with better pay and fewer hours."

"Awww," said Jillian.

"What?" said Megan.

"We do hard work."

Megan threw her skirt on the floor and said, "Jillian."

Her boyfriend, Randy, was making dinner. He was cutting a zucchini into slices and laying the slices on top of a frozen cheese pizza.

"Today she burped in the middle of a sentence," said Megan. "Like it was a word in her sentence."

"Ha ha," said Randy. Megan leaned against the kitchen sink.

"JILLIAN!" said Megan, raising her arms.

"Yeesh," said Randy.

"She thinks she's going to become a personal organizer."

"I don't know what that is," said Randy.

"Yes you do."

"Yeah, I guess I do," said Randy.

"When she told me about it, it occurred to me to say, 'Well, never in all my life!'"

Megan thought about this and tried to sit on the edge of the sink. "I don't really know why I wanted to say that. I just want to do my work without having to listen to her dreams." Megan gestured again. "I don't want to stress out about her dreams."

"It's a really small office, right?" her boyfriend asked. "So, you're really trapped in there."

"Completely trapped."

Megan kept thinking about Jillian and tried to sit on the edge of the sink, but fell backward into it. She hit her head on the aluminum cabinets. Randy heard this, along with the noise of some dishes.

"You all right?" asked Randy.

Randy walked to the sink, which was attached to the wall shared with the living room. Megan started shaking and said she thought she might throw up. He put his arms around her and lifted her out of the sink. When he looked down into the sink, he cringed.

"I fell on that knife," said Megan.

"You sure did," said Randy.

He walked her through the living room while assuring her that she would be fine. Megan's knees jiggled.

"Here, lie down," he said. Megan got on her stomach on the bed and Randy pulled her tights down. He looked over at the pile of clothing in the corner of their small, unlit bedroom, hoping to see a pair of sweatpants in the wad.

"I'm going to get something for this," he said.

"Did I cut myself?" asked Megan.

"You did," he said.

"I thought so," she said, and then nearly fainted.

Randy got up from his squat beside the bed and walked to the kitchen. Megan continued to lie on the bed on her stomach, her face pointed at the clothing wad. In the kitchen, where he was getting a bowl of warm water and a roll of masking tape, Randy saw the knife she'd sat on. It was surrounded by watery blood. Next to the knife, floating in a teacup, was a small crouton.

He went to the bathroom to dry-heave and get gauze, Neosporin, and Tylenol.

When he got back to the bedroom, she was sobbing. He set his things on the nightstand and took a moment to look at the underwear around Megan's ankles.

"Hey, it's not that bad," he said. The gash was deep, but not incredibly bloody. He rinsed and dried it, then covered it with a quarter of the tube of Neosporin.

"It really hurts," she said.

"I know, I know," he said. He rubbed her head for a minute. "Do you still want me to make that pizza?"

"What? No. Maybe. Maybe I'll want that pizza later," she said. "You decide, I don't know."

"Okay, I'll decide," he said. He wiped her nose and eyes

with the extra gauze. She looked like a disgusting dead sea creature. Randy began to smile and wipe the stray hairs out of her face.

"My ass hurts so much," she sobbed.

"I know it does, honey," he said.

Megan remembered what she had been talking about when she slid into the sink and said, "Jillian is such a fucking idiot!"

"I know, honey," said Randy. "She's a total idiot."

"No, I'm serious," she cried. "This is serious!"

"Of course it is," said Randy.

"I get a dangerous sense of foreboding when I'm around her." Megan swallowed some spit. "She's seeping into me! Everything she says and does, whenever she opens her mouth!"

Randy nodded and rubbed Megan's ears. "I know."

"But I won't let her get to me."

"That's good. You should really try to let this all go, it's not good for you. You talk about her every day. I'm so happy you're going to brush it off, that's really mature."

Megan omitted his statement from her mind. "I'll turn the tables," she said. "I'll enjoy it. Every stupid idea she has is mine now. I'll savor it, that's what I'll do."

Randy frowned and balled up the snot gauze before tossing it onto the nightstand.

The bus pulled up to the eight-story medical building and Megan had her usual fantasy about remaining onboard until the end of the line, but she heaved herself toward the doors of the bus anyway. Slumping along, sort of throwing her feet one after the other, she crossed the street, entered the building, rode the elevator, walked down the hallway, and then stood facing her office door. She stared at it. Then she went inside and there was Jillian.

"Hey, Miss Megan!"

"Hey," said Megan.

"How was your night, do anything fun? Anything new?"

"Nothing's really changed since yesterday, no," said Megan. Megan put her knee on her chair and opened Citrix, the intranet portal that connected her office with the hospital. Citrix was complex and opaque, and to understand it fully a person would probably need to attend a three-day regional seminar. Megan entered her secret username, "Megan," and her secret password, "password."

"Well, if you don't have any news, let me tell you about my crazy night." Jillian separated out the words "crazy" and "night." Megan tried to ease her weight slowly down on her injured haunch.

"I am going to get a dog and start my own business," said Jillian.

"Oh yeah?" said Megan.

"Oh yeah. Do you want to see the dog?"

Megan did not want to see the dog, but she agreed anyway. She walked the two paces to Jillian's desk and stood there with her arms crossed. Let's see this fucking dog, you fucking moron.

"She's a special needs puppy," breathed Jillian. "And she's

dog of the day. It's a two-hundred-dollar adoption fee. I don't really have that much, but I want her so, so bad. Isn't she cute?"

They both took a second to admire the dog. Megan thought it was a completely idiotic idea. She was, in some ways, ethically opposed to pet ownership.

"Yeah, she's cute. But the adoption fees are to make sure the new owners can afford dog food and vet bills." Megan cleared her throat and walked back to her desk. Her foot slipped out of her shoe. "And, if she really is a *special needs* dog, you know the vet bills are gonna be high. Just saying, might not be the best dog for you. Or, maybe it's not the best time to get a dog. You have to plan for that stuff."

"Yeah, well, I'm pretty sure my little boy really wants a dog, and I think the most important thing for a special needs dog to have is love."

Oh my god, this dog is going to die within a week, thought Megan.

"Oh, and I have to tell you about my idea to work from home."

Just as a thought experiment, Megan scanned the room for potential weapons. Jillian's voice came in and out of focus.

". . . software I can . . . medical coding from . . . that cool?? . . . I can take . . . little companion!"

Megan's cut was starting to scab, but the scab was still thin and new—that kind of yellow, crystallized pus, like dried snot or eye-crap. It cracked a little when Megan put weight on it.

"It's going to be so great. I can't wait for summer. I'm

gonna work from home, and I'm gonna have a dog on a leash and my baby's hand in mine," said Jillian. Megan glanced over her shoulder and confirmed that, yes, Jillian did have a faraway look on her face.

"Yep. This summer's gonna be the best," said Megan.

Megan started filing the images from the colonoscopies performed the day before. The large volume of documents suggested a kind of drive-through approach to the procedures that Megan found tactless. The images in the folder were the same as they always were. Each patient was represented by a grid of two-by-two-inch photographs of twisting, ribbed tunnels, which were sometimes pink and slick, but sometimes filled with crust, sludge, blood, or little hangy-balls of bowel skin. The one thing she never saw in any of these photos was waste, but sometimes she came across a report with no images and the ghastly description "patient failed to empty completely, reschedule procedure."

"Hi," said Jillian. "I'm calling about the software package I saw on your website.... Yuh-huh. Yeah, I'm really, um, really interested in it. Yes, ma'am, I am starting my own coding business. Yes, ma'am, medical coding. Yes, I will. Okay. You want me to give you my number?"

Jillian hung up the phone and sighed, thrilled. "Oh, dude, Megan, this is going to be so awesome!"

"Huh?" said Megan.

Jillian gasped. "Oh, I almost forgot! We have twelve patients this afternoon, so get ready! I made up some new registration forms." Megan could feel that Jillian was approaching her.

Jillian opened a manila folder under Megan's face and said, "It's basically the same as the last one, except for here." She double-tapped. Jillian's fingers seemed to get a great sensory thrill from paper, judging by the way they touched it.

"And this is the new confidentiality agreement."

"I got it, Jillian," said Megan. "Thank you. Thank you for doing this."

"Oh, and since you were late again today, I took your missed calls. You had *lots*. Let me get those notes for you."

"Thank you very much," said Megan.

The doctors arrived ten minutes later, and Megan gave them both a curt, nonverbal greeting. Jillian showed them both the dog.

Later, Jillian received a phone call. Megan observed an immediate shift in tone. Her ears perked.

"No, I'm sorry but that's not fair," said Jillian. "It's not fair, and it's incorrect." Pause. "No."

Megan shifted the weight off her left butt cheek and jiggled her mouse, miming work, but alert to the conversation.

"They told me I didn't need to pay it." Jillian paused. "Well, I lost their name, this was three years ago."

Ah, the fabled "they." Megan smiled.

"No, I didn't get it in writing. Well, I guess I'm a trusting person." Pause. "Ma'am, I feel like it's very inappropriate for you to contact me at my place of work. I can give you a fax number where you can send me more information, and I will look into it."

Megan knew what that really meant.

"What? You expect me to pay you nine dollars to send me

a form that I'm going to use to pay you two hundred dollars?" Jillian made choking and scoffing noises while she listened to the person on the other end and Megan's black heart swelled with glee.

"I really feel like you're taking advantage of me right now and, ma'am, I have a child to take care of and I'm about to get a dog and I have too many expenses right now to pay you nine dollars, let alone two hundred dollars."

Jillian was becoming clearly angry.

"I am unable to pay over the phone, but I can send you a money order at my earliest convenience. No, I don't have a credit card. No. No, I don't have a debit card. I don't have a checking account." Pause. "Well, you know what, someone was stealing my identity so that's why I don't have one anymore. Yes, I got that taken care of. I will try to send you that money order as soon as I can, but I think you're being very unfair and rude. Yes, ma'am."

Jillian let out a stifled scream at the phone after she hung it up, then laughed and said, "My car."

"Hmm?" said Megan.

"I got a ticket last night for running a red light on my way home and I, you know, didn't have my license on me, so the cop looked me up in his thingy, and it turned out I have an unpaid fine from an accident I had three years ago. I got bad injuries. Apparently, my license has been suspended for three years, and now I have to pay this frickin' fine."

"Geez," said Megan.

"Yeah. I'm not even supposed to be driving right now, so I have to be real careful on my way home."

"Yeah, make sure to be real careful," said Megan.

The patients started coming in.

Jillian said "Noooo problem!" a lot.

Megan said "Sure" a lot.

During downtime Jillian would look at the internet, but sometimes she would just sit and stare at the wall.

Jillian sat at her desk practicing visualizations, as had been suggested to her by a few members of her church group. When someone opened the door, she thought *"Action!"* and then her face would become bright and her voice would flow easily out of her mouth and she could say "Oh, hi, how are you?" as if she had no real problems of her own. This ticket thing would not do. That stupid woman at the court office telling her she had to pay nine dollars to get a special form to attach to the money order to get the hold taken off her license. I spent nine dollars on lunch today, she thought. I'm not going to spend nine dollars on a piece of paper. And Miss Prissy Prim Tight Lips Megan over there on the other side of the office, what was her problem? But I will have that dog, she said to herself, because the dog was part of the visualization she was doing. Where do you want to see yourself in half a year? In half a year I want to see myself walking down the sidewalk with this internet dog, Carla. Carla would be an okay name. Walking down the sidewalk with Carla, the dog of the day, practically a famous dog. How silly. But this dog was essential, and this dog cost as much as the fine she had to pay as a result of an accident she'd been seriously injured in, and the court should pay her, in her opinion, not the other way around.

For the visualizations, she knew she was supposed to pick something that went good with her personality, so that's why the dog made sense. She was a mother, a nurturer. Also, being a mother meant you had a kid to entertain, which meant you had to give it something to play with, which was why (another reason why) the dog made sense. And she lived outside the city, in an apartment, yes, but still outside the city, and she'd heard city dogs weren't that happy. She knew she wasn't going to pick something like "become a rock star in half a year" even though she'd had a pretty good voice as a kid—ha ha!— and kind of a rock star's appetites, if you know what I mean. And that would be a good reason to not pick rock star, too. That was her old life and personality. Now she was MOM and WORKER (not just worker, but office manager, since Miss Tight Lips had no interest in advancement, it seemed) and a dog would suit her just fine, so she would get Carla, and a month from now that dog would be frolicking in the medians at the end of her leash.

She would not use a choke collar, obviously.

The workday ended, and Jillian drove home quickly, but still carefully, in her beige four-door sedan because, on one hand, she needed to get to her home phone before the Humane Society closed, but on the other hand she knew she didn't have any more gimmes.

Her car had little piles of white paper coffee cups and magazines that had been stepped on and twisted into spirals. Everything was covered in a layer of crushed Apple Jacks. Some books lay on their spines or sides or wherever they landed, books about confidence and stuff, which she knew were super corny, but helped her out and helped her stay on track. Jillian felt like she was gliding home in a star craft, she was so excited. She glided into the day-care parking lot and landed her craft in the spot just next to the handicapped spot, swooped through the doors, and looked through that teeming mass of children to find hers, that little halfie. Half hers, you know.

"Hey, Barb!" said Jillian to the day-care teacher.

"Adam!" shouted Barb, and then Adam walked casually out of a little plastic house.

At home, Jillian handed Adam the remote and said, "Now, you sit in here. Mommy's gotta go do something."

"Can we eat soon?" asked Adam.

"Oh yeah, dinner's soon, just watch your show for a second." It was a documentary about baby animals that Adam seemed to like.

Jillian walked to the kitchen, picked up the cordless, picked up the laptop, walked to her bedroom, and shut the door. It was so exciting, ugh! She dialed the Humane Society and looked at the picture of Carla. The phone rang twice before it was answered. Each step was a thrill.

"Hi!" said Jillian. "I'm calling to inquire about the dog on your website named Carla, the special needs dog?"

"Oooohh, I'm sorry, but Carla was adopted yesterday."

"Oh, really? Are you sure? Because she's still up on your web page."

"Yeah, I'm sure. Every time we put up one of those photos the dogs get adopted almost the same day. It really makes people fall in love, I guess."

"Yeah, I guess it does," said Jillian. "Well, maybe you should take it down so you don't give a misrepresentation of the dogs you actually do have."

"We have a lot of wonderful dogs in right now. All the time, in fact. Do you want to know our hours?"

"No, not really, I only wanted Carla."

"Are you sure? Carla's not our only special needs dog, if that's what you're looking for."

"I'll think about it."

"Okay, well, please keep us in mind," said the woman.

"Bye."

Jillian clicked the *end* button on the cordless and sat on the edge of her bed for a second. Then she put a pillow to her face and screamed "fuck" three times.

She set the pillow down, punched it twice, and then said "Mommy's all right!" and went back to the living room.

"And my boss was like, 'We have to get this,'" said Carrie. "So we walked up to the guy and my boss was like, 'I'll give you fifty dollars for that llama,' and he did it."

"Oh my god, that's hilarious," said Jessica. "Steve, check out this llama at Carrie's desk." Jessica handed the phone to Steve. Everyone was smiling.

"That's a life-size llama," said Steve.

"We had to carry it back to our office on the bus," said Carrie. "It almost didn't fit through the door, that's how big it was. We almost hit the bus driver in the face with it, that's how big it was." A few people laughed. Carrie reached out for the phone. "Here." She flipped to the next picture. "That's how big it is." The photo showed Carrie and the llama, Carrie with her arm around the llama, Carrie wearing glasses and grinning, the llama looking dingy and staring with its dead eyes at the camera, the two of them in Carrie's well-lit office.

"Oh my god, you look so tiny next to that llama," said Jessica.

Peering over Bill's shoulder, Megan could see that Carrie had lots of nice plants in her office.

"I'm so lucky. I love my boss and I love my office," said Carrie, reaching again for her phone. She gave the photo of herself a little smile before putting it away.

Megan looked across the party and saw Randy by the bathroom. She was trapped between Jessica and a coffee table. To get to Randy would require her to either step over the coffee table or ask Jessica to press herself against the wall, and Jessica looked like she was having a nice time.

"Well," said Carrie. "I have some cool news."

It would be rude to interrupt Jessica's good time.

"You know that magazine *Dale Carnegie*? They're doing a thirty under thirty thing next issue."

And it would really look like she was a wild animal or something if she tried to climb over the table. And plus her ass still hurt, so it wouldn't be graceful. She'd have to limp her way out of the corner.

"Do we know any of the thirty under thirty?" Bill asked.

"I'll say," said Carrie. She was being cheeky.

A girl named Annie walked up to their small group and said, "Hey! Sorry, I was eavesdropping. Is it you? Are you one of the thirty under thirty?"

Carrie nodded.

Megan reached into her purse and took out another beer, her third. The sound of the tab cracking was, she thought, a nice contribution. Cheers! She drank very quickly.

Annie took out a cigarette and said, "That's awesome." Annie and Megan had met before. Megan cleared her throat.

"Hey, Annie, can I have one of those?" she asked.

"Oh, sure," said Annie.

"Randy has mine. I can pay you back later."

"Oh, don't worry about it. Really."

Annie passed her a Camel and then held out her pink lighter, already lit. Megan had to dip her head into the middle of the conversation, which had stopped, maybe pointedly, to light her smoke out of Annie's hand. Megan straightened, leaving behind a plume of smoke.

"Thanks," she said.

"It's cool. I feel like I haven't seen you in a while, Megan. What have you been up to?" asked Annie.

Everyone was still being quiet and staring, which didn't really feel polite.

"Well, I cut my ass on a knife in the kitchen sink."

It was uncomfortable to have four people looking at her and listening to what she was saying. She took a drink of beer while Annie laughed a little and said, "What?"

"I fell in the sink on a knife and cut my ass."

"Oh my god, are you all right?"

"Sure," said Megan.

"Did you have to go to the doctor?"

"Nah," said Megan. "Now that it's over, it's kind of funny."

"Hmm," said Annie. Her face communicated that she didn't really think it was that funny.

"Hey," said Megan, looking at Jessica. "Could I get by you? I have to pee."

"Okay, sure."

"Thanks for the cigarette," Megan said to Annie. Annie forced a smile and waved.

On her way to the bathroom, Megan stopped by Randy. She whispered, "Carrie can roll it up and stick it in her prim little asshole."

"Jesus Christ," said Randy. Prim little asshole.

There was a line for the bathroom.

The tall guy in front of her said, "So you're in the line, too, huh?"

"Yeah," said Megan. She covered her mouth to burp and opened another beer.

"Sucks. This always happens at these things," said the guy.

"Yeah, well. It's an apartment. They don't usually have more than one bathroom."

"You want to come in with me? I could pee in the tub if you really need to go."

"No, I'm good, thanks," said Megan.

"Hey, man, I was just offering, okay?"

"Yeah, I know, it's fine."

"You don't have to act like an asshole about it."

"Well, I don't really think I'm being an asshole. I just don't, uh, I don't really have to go that bad."

"Then why are you in the bathroom line? There are people who actually have to go, you know."

Megan looked behind her and saw no one.

"I just think I can wait, that's all."

"What kind of accent is that?" asked the guy.

"What do you mean? I don't have an accent."

"Yes you do. Are you a liar?"

"I mean . . . I'm from Michigan."

"You have a foreign accent," said the guy, and then the bathroom door opened. "Ladies first."

"No, really, go ahead," said Megan. "Allow me to do this one thing for you." The guy snorted. He was in and out in a minute, he didn't wash his hands. When he got out of the bathroom, he held the door open for her and bowed a little.

Megan locked the door behind her, washed her hands, then pulled down her pants. There were no leaks on the bandage and she decided to leave it alone. She pulled her pants back up, finished her beer, and looked at herself in the mirror.

"Hello," she said to herself before leaving. "Hello, darling."

Amanda, a familiar face from school, was in the kitchen looking in the refrigerator.

"Hey, familiar face, I have beer," said Megan.

"Phew!" said Amanda. Amanda was nice to Megan and she had an unpretentious look. Amanda was low-medium pretty, less pretty than Megan, which put Megan at ease, but more attractive than Megan because she bothered to groom herself. Megan observed that Amanda's level of grooming was not too high, though, and then she felt guilty for gauging her comfort with Amanda by such idiotic standards. Megan reached into her purse and handed Amanda a beer.

"How many beers do you have in there?"

Megan looked in her bag and said, "Used to be twenty-four, but now I'm not sure."

"Ha ha ha, you're nuts."

"Oh, I'm nuts," said Megan. "I'm a regular nut."

"So, what's up? How's work?"

"Work is . . . I spend thirty-two hours a week with a woman who isn't allowed to cut her hangnails for religious reasons. Vanity or something. We listen to light Christian rock together all day. She forwards me photo threads of baby animals with affirmations at the bottom and she belches all the time."

Amanda laughed and said "Gee whiz." Megan shrugged and offered up a cheers.

There was that kind of pause that happens when one person is trying to think of something interesting to say while the other person waits. Megan grimaced and said, "I'm not that interesting."

Amanda laughed again. Then she became serious and said, "Hey, are you going to look for something else? You seem pretty unhappy."

"Ehh, I don't know. I've looked, and I usually end up feeling pretty overwhelmed and underqualified for all of the interesting jobs, and then I have a thought spiral, and then I feel like I made a bad move somewhere back in middle school, and then I feel like there's no hope at all for me and then I contemplate suicide."

Amanda rolled her eyes in a friendly way and said, "I know what you mean, but it's not that big of a deal. You just apply for stuff. And fake it."

"I'm just trying to live pure," said Megan. "Ambition's for the devil."

At that moment, Carrie walked up and gave Amanda a hug and said, "Oh my god, girl!" Megan opened another beer and put the empty back in her purse. "I've got to show you this llama my boss and I bought off a homeless guy."

"Ha ha ha," said Amanda, taking Carrie's phone. "It's enormous! Megan, have you seen this?"

"Yeah, I've seen it."

"Hey, can I get a cigarette?" asked Carrie.

"Oh, sure," said Amanda. "You want one?"

"Yeah, thanks," said Megan.

"I quit," said Carrie. "I quit smoking and I quit coffee, and I feel so much better now."

"How long have you been not smoking?" asked Amanda, handing Carrie her lighter.

"Like, three weeks. Have you ever quit before?"

"I take breaks sometimes," said Amanda.

"It's just this really clean feeling, like I can feel everything that's dead inside of me coming to life again. I can feel life flowing through me." Carrie held her hands out, palms up, and flexed her fingers like claws. The cigarette was between her right pointer and middle fingers. Megan raised her eyebrows at the floor.

"Except when I'm drinking, then I can't help it," said Carrie.

"You're fine just as long as you don't buy your own pack," said Megan.

"Exactly," said Carrie, looking at Megan for the first time all evening. "Hey, do you have anything to drink?" she asked Amanda.

"No, I got this beer from Megan."

Carrie looked at Megan with a dumb expression.

"Take your pick," said Megan, holding the bag out to her.

"Oh my god, there are like twelve empty cans in here."

It was true. Megan smelled like beer and had been trailing a little dribble of lukewarm beer behind her all night.

"I'm from Michigan," said Megan. "I take them back across the border for the deposit money."

"Ha ha ha," said Amanda.

"That's disgusting," said Carrie, but she reached into the sack anyway. "So, what is that, like a dollar twenty in cans?"

Megan shrugged.

"So, how have you been?" asked Amanda.

"Pretty good, pretty good," said Carrie. "I have so many projects going on right now that my head is like," she bugged her eyeballs and held her hands on either side of her head.

While they were talking about having too many interesting things to do, Randy and two of his friends walked up to their circle.

Randy whispered, "Can I have a beer?"

"Can I have a cigarette?"

They traded.

"You should try some of David's growler," said Randy.

Megan shook her head. "Never mix, never worry."

"They're both beer," he said.

Megan turned to him and said very quietly, "This is killing me," and then she walked out of the kitchen.

When it was time to wind things down, Megan was sitting on the couch with the guy from the bathroom line. Megan spotted Carrie and said, "Hey, Carrie! Come over here. Hey, this is the girl I was telling you about with the llama. Hey, Carrie, come show this guy the picture of you with the llama."

"Um, I really have to go," said Carrie.

"She's got this picture of herself with a llama the size of a young woman trapped inside of an enormous stuffed llama," said Megan. "And she's embracing it with one arm and she's smiling at the camera." Megan mimicked Carrie unfavorably. She made a peace sign.

"That sounds cool," said the guy.

"She and her boss got it off of an *untouchable*." She whisper-yelled the word "untouchable."

Carrie rolled her eyes and said, "Okay, bye, guys." Megan said a few more things.

"Time to go home," said Randy, helping her up from the couch.

"Why is everyone such a fucking asshole?" she asked.

"What do you mean? Who's an asshole?"

"Why is *everyone* I said." Megan's knees buckled. She palmed the ground. "I hate Carrie. She repulses me." Randy hoisted her up by the arm, the way people do with toddlers.

"Come on, she's not repulsive. I can see how she might be kind of intimidating. She used to intimidate me a little."

"I didn't say *intimidating*, I said *repulsive. Intimidating* would imply that there was some reason I should feel inferior to her, but I don't feel inferior because her life is a lie and she's got no heart."

Randy laughed a little. "Okay."

"She's got no heart!" she bellowed.

"Okay," said Randy.

Megan straightened herself, rolled her eyes, chuckled, and said, "Soooo typical, sooo typical," not knowing quite what she meant.

4

The next morning the alarm went off at seven-thirty. Randy pushed Megan to the edge of the bed with his foot.

"You know, I think it's probably okay for me to get a few more hours of sleep. It might even be dangerous or unethical for me to go to work like this," she said.

"Get up," said Randy.

"The cruelty, the inhumanity," Megan mumbled.

She swung her torso upright and pushed herself off the bed and walked to the bathroom, placed towels around the base of the claw-foot tub (all original!) to absorb the leaks, and then turned on the faucet.

In the shower, as soon as her muscles began to relax and as soon as she started to feel fresh and as if the bearing of the day might be fractionally possible, she heard that old familiar voice—possibly her own voice, it was so familiar—whisper something awful. This morning it whispered "llama" and she burst into tears as her amnesia was lifted. Megan groan-screamed and sputtered something about wishing to be put out of her misery, all while scrubbing her armpits with a teal-colored shower poof. The last mild dignity of her wailing was interrupted by a diarrhea feeling that usually followed a long night of drinking canned, watery beer.

"Oh, great."

She scrubbed all of her dark, fetid cracks—ass, snatch, and toes—blew her nose in the direction of the drain, and then rinsed herself with cold water. She almost fell as she got out of the tub and was not surprised by this, in the same way she was not surprised by the bawling and the indigestion. She dried herself, flossed, put on lotion, and took the obligatory five min-utes to comb through her hair (a new habit), then wrapped her hair in the towel. There were few more vulnerable feelings to Megan than taking a nasty shit while wet, cold, slimy, and naked. Under ideal conditions she would have put her pajamas back on before unleashing, but she had slept in her clothes.

It was always the smell of burning tires that rose from the bowl beneath her on these kinds of mornings. Better than vomiting, always, *always* better than vomiting, though. At least while shitting she had a chance to daydream. She flushed, rewashed her ass and crotch (also a new habit, preceded by a three-year yeast infection), washed her hands, put some Neosporin on the thick scab on her ass, shook her hair out of the towel, then wrapped the towel around her body.

"Hey, baby, you look cute," said Randy.

"Yeah I feel fucking adorable, where are my tights?" He doesn't know where my tights are, where the fuck are my fucking tights? she thought. She found them. She put them on with a skirt and a sweater because if she dressed well they might not notice. She blow-dried her hair.

The cigarette and the coffee and the bagel were carrots to lure her out of her apartment. Yeah, I'm like a little horsey, she thought. The cigarette went in her mouth as soon as she left her apartment building, and its smoke made her sick and almost made her swoon. She had smoked too many last night, but she had also not had a cigarette in about five hours. After a cup of coffee, she knew all of her body would clench and her mind would feel elevated (ah, yesyesyesyes, *elevated*) and her midday cigarette would nicely diffuse the caffeine tension. She knew that cigarette would be the best of the day.

She rinsed her mouth with the coffee on the nauseating bus ride. She'd eaten the bagel at the bus stop. She knew, later, she would have to secretly pocket the public restroom key and then make up some excuse to leave the office. Better they think I'm slacking off than taking a dump, she thought and then laughed.

Llama.

Morning came, as usual, at 0600 hours for Jillian. She felt good and hungry (some mornings she woke up feeling full, and those were not usually good days) and her bed was warm. For the first two minutes of each day, she felt like an actual normal living thing with manageable tasks. But then her brain would whisper the words "every morning is an opportunity waiting to happen," and, behind that phrase, she would know there were things she had done wrong, there were people who were against her, and there was generally a lot of disappointment in her life. She would sit on the edge of her bed and look at the window, which faced another window of an apartment across the courtyard. Sometimes she had time to shower, but it wasn't always important.

She poured Adam some Apple Jacks and picked him up out of his bed, set him down in the kitchen, and then watched him eat. He didn't even open his eyes. He was hilarious.

Since black coffee was disgusting, Jillian liked to get a Starbucks on her drive to work. She knew she could save money if she made her own, but there was a drive-through right past Adam's day care, and it was good to have a treat, so she treated herself. The downside was it gave her heartburn.

When she got to work, Jillian microwaved the remainder of her Starbucks and opened her email.

"Oh, this is cute," she said.

On the computer screen there was an email from Sister Grace about how dogs were better people than people. *Enjoy this, I know I did* 😊*!!!!!!!!!!* it said.

"This is real cute." Jillian hit *forward* and selected twenty of her contacts.

The door opened.

"Hey, Megan!" said Jillian.

"Hi," said Megan.

"I just sent you an email."

"Okay."

"It's nothing serious, but it's real cute, okay?"

"Okay, let me turn on my computer."

She's going to like this, thought Jillian.

"Do I have any messages so far?" asked Megan.

"Nope, phones haven't started ringing just yet," said Jillian. "So, what's new with you?"

"Nothing." Megan felt awkward for saying it that way. "I mean, nothing's really changed since yesterday. How was your night?"

"It was good. I think I'm going to hold off on getting that dog."

Megan opened her email and saw the thing from Jillian.

"Two hundred dollars is too much for an adoption fee. I just don't think I feel okay paying it," said Jillian.

"Yeah, well, I know I wouldn't want a dog. Seems like it would be really inhibiting if you wanted to go on vacation or have friends, or inhibiting financially at least, if you want to be able to pay your bills. That's what the adoption fee is for. To weed people out."

"Yeah, well, I guess I just thought my son would like having a dog."

"Right," said Megan.

"Anyway, nothing new with you, then?"

"Nope. Nothing at all." Megan's hangover was critical.

"You get your email?" asked Jillian.

"Yeah, I got it. Cute dogs."

"I know, I just thought that was so funny."

I just want to get my work done so I can go home, thought Megan. And then what?

Things are going to get better after a while, after I get a few more things in order and out of the way, things are going to start getting better, I promise, thought Jillian. I promise.

Dr. Billings poked his head out of his office. "Uh, Jillian," he said. "Did you get a chance to order those gowns?"

"Yeah, I ordered them last week when you asked me to."

"They haven't come yet. Usually it only takes a few days. They're in town. If you haven't ordered them yet, I could always drive by after work."

"No, I ordered them. I don't know why they haven't come yet, but I ordered them."

"Okay. If they don't come tomorrow, why don't you give them a call. They might not have the right address, but they should have our address."

"No problem," said Jillian. Megan rolled her eyes. "I'll give 'em a call tomorrow," said Jillian.

"Okay. I don't have patients until one, right?" asked Dr. Billings.

"Nope, that's right," said Jillian.

"Okay," said Dr. Billings. "I'll be back." He left the office. Jillian picked up the phone and in a moment whispered, "Hi, my name is Jillian and I'm calling from Dr. Billings' office. Yeah. Hi. I'd like to place an order for some surgical gowns. You got it."

Megan paused from her work and shook her head. I'm shaking my head with disbelief, she thought. But then she realized an opportunity had been presented to her, and she slipped the public restroom key into the waistband of her skirt and went outside for a smoke break.

The cigarette undid her tension from the top down, liquefying her brain, lungs, fingers, bowels, spirit, etc.

In the locked single-toilet public restroom, between spasms, she leaned back on the flush pipe and thought.

"Do you have a name for that llama yet?"

"No, I don't have a name yet."

"Why don't you name it Megan?"

"Uuuhhmmm?"

"Yeah, you can name it Megan and then you can take a knife and stab it in the ass or the face or wherever you want. Whatever you want, really, but if you name it Megan it'll be like I'm close to you while you work."

"Uh, what?"

"Not that I want to be near you. You know I don't like you, right?"

"Uh, what?"

"I just think it would be pleasant to have some kind of non-sentient representation of myself floating out there in the world."

"I'm sorry?"

"You know, *not sentient*? Like it doesn't have any self-awareness or consciousness? The llama?"

"Yeah, I know what the word means."

"Oh, right, you went to grad school. I forgot you went to grad school."

Megan wiped and flushed and tried to use the flush sound to symbolically rid herself of the fantasy of saying something to Carrie about the llama.

"Show this guy a picture of your llama," she said while she washed her hands. "Show this guy that picture of your llama."

Since it would make her feel better, she let herself cry whenever she wanted to. She put her head in her arms and her arms on the bathroom wall. When she finished, she washed her face and shook her fist at her reflection.

"I'll get YOU!" said Megan.

God, I'm hilarious, she thought.

She walked back down the hallway and the hallway didn't exist.

Everything about her life was so much the same from day to day that it almost didn't exist.

Randy didn't get what the big deal was about Jillian. He didn't think she sounded like a liar, and he thought Megan was blowing things out of proportion. He'd suggested this once.

"Megan, do you think you're redirecting your dissatisfaction with your job onto Jillian?"

She'd said, "Fuck you."

Randy was sitting at his computer desk at home. He was confident that Megan's Carrie thing was fleeting, despite her display last night, and he decided not to edit himself to accommodate her.

Megan opened the door.

"Hey," said Randy.

Megan slipped out of her bag, coat, and shoes and then took off her skirt, tights, underpants, sweater, and bra on her walk to the bedroom. She got into pajamas, put her hair in a stupid-looking ponytail, and said "Hey" as she sat down at the kitchen table.

Randy started by mentioning some design work of Carrie's that he'd seen.

"Hmm," said Megan.

He had the magazine he'd seen it in, and he brought it to her, opened to the correct page. He took a seat.

"Oh, wow," said Megan. She picked up the magazine and dropped it back down on the table.

"I think it's really cool," said Randy.

"Sure. It looks like everything else, if that's what you mean by *cool*."

"No, I mean, this is really professional work. It's cool that it's done by someone we know."

"Is it?"

"Yes."

"It's just a formula. I don't feel honored to know a formula. Only one in, I don't know, ten thousand designers is a real artist. I don't know any designers who've been artists since Bauhaus, and they were fighting Nazis with their designs, not . . . imported produce or whatever."

Randy straightened. "Well, anyway, I was thinking it would be fun to ask Carrie to help me do some web design, and I wanted to ask if you thought her stuff would translate well to a website."

Megan scratched her face. "Yeah. It'd translate well to a website, if that's all you're thinking about. But you could do this kind of stuff alone," she said, gesturing at the magazine. "I mean, well, to me, the real hindrance in working with her—or anyone like her—would be the total hypocrisy of it all. Encouraging someone who considers herself to be a forerunning mind of our generation while all she's doing is, essentially, coloring in the lines would make me, personally, want to fucking kill myself."

Randy stared at her.

"What?" she said.

"I don't see what Carrie does as hypocritical."

"Oh, you used to agree with me. What, now that I'm applying the same idea to your precious darling Carrie, you don't agree with me about how stupidly pretentious all of these graphic design assholes are, with their fucking letterpressed business cards with their WordPress addresses on them? Playing around and being condescending about creative recycling and community-based whatever-the-fuck? Help me help you, Randy."

Megan paused.

"I'm sure they all shampoo their pubes," she said.

"I'm only talking about this one spread."

"It's hollow."

"You know, that's kind of what I do for a living."

"It's different."

"Is it? I do web design for a living, and I like it. You're talking about what I do. And, anyway, you buy organic produce."

"Yeah, but I don't kid myself that it's a part of a movement I'm involved in. I know it's just groceries. That self-important look in their eyes makes me puke."

"Okay, so you don't think I should work with her."

"Do what you want, but I just think you or any fucking monkey with a reference image and a laptop could do what she does. I mean, all she really did was finish her homework. She's not some kind of magic fairy genius."

"Nobody thinks she's a magic fairy genius," said Randy.

"You say that now."

"And why wouldn't I want to work with someone who finished their homework? Or a magic fairy, for that matter?"

Not having a direct answer to this, Megan began the painful process of shutting the fuck up. The psychological resistance she felt was intense enough to have a physical counterpart, which was a grating feeling in the center of her chest.

"No, you're right," she said. "I'm sorry. I guess I just had a bad day. I don't know why I'm ranting."

She sat on the floor at Randy's feet and put her head in his lap.

"How's your butt?" he asked.

"Itchy."

"How's your head?"

"Horrible."

"How was your day?"

"Uuuunnnnghghg. You know how when you drink a lot, the next morning you usually feel depressed? Just, like, chemically, because your body's in withdrawal?"

"Well . . . yeah."

"Or maybe it's because your body gives off an excess of serotonin when you're drunk, so in the morning you have depleted serotonin."

"Is that how you feel?"

"Yeah, but I'm pretty sure it's just a body thing. There must be some chemical reason why I keep replaying the night." She had a biting memory. "Over and over. Because I didn't really do anything that bad. But you know that feeling where you replay and then edit the conversations you had and then you feel really vulnerable and like everyone hates you, even though you didn't do anything that out of the ordinary?"

"Yeah, I know that feeling. It's a sugar crash or something."

"I feel so stupid about that llama thing at the end of the night."

"What? I'm sure Carrie doesn't care, and I thought it was funny. It was funny."

"She thinks I'm so disgusting."

"No. She doesn't think you're disgusting, Megan. She doesn't think like that."

Megan started crying.

"Oh, come on, what? What?"

Megan kept crying, and Randy kept saying "What?"

"I wish you'd say something," said Randy.

Megan's throat squeezed shut every time she almost started saying something. She opened her mouth, which he couldn't see with her head in his lap, then closed it, opened it, then closed it.

"Come on," he said.

"What do you mean she doesn't think like that?" Megan shouted. "I think like that. I think she's disgusting and you know it, you know I think like that, so what do you mean she doesn't think like that? What, do you think I should just go ahead and try to be more like Carrie? Should I get myself some abstract ambitions and start designing events calendars?"

"Oh, come on."

Megan wailed.

She's not always like this, thought Randy. "Why are you being like this?" he asked.

"Because I'm dying!" she said. Then she stopped crying.

"Here. Let me get you a Kleenex," said Randy, scooting out from under her head.

She sat up straight and mucus ran down her face.

"Here," said Randy. He handed her a tissue.

Megan felt like an idiot, but she also felt a little better. She was embarrassed and got up from the floor without making eye contact with Randy. She walked to the bathroom while blowing her nose. Randy sat back down.

"I look like a Harlequin Baby," shouted Megan. Randy started laughing. Megan started laughing. Megan came out of the bathroom and looked at Randy.

"I'm still mad at you," said Megan.

"Why?"

"Because you love Carrie the turd."

Randy winced and said, "Come on."

Later, he brought her juice and Tylenol in bed. He didn't want to feel like they were arguing anymore.

"How's Jillian?" he asked. A peace offering.

Megan sighed. "She continues to be a thick strand in the malevolent web of my daily routine."

5

Jillian and her baby were sitting on the couch having dinner and Jillian felt hollow like she sometimes did. Just a body thing, really. They were watching *America's Funniest Home Videos*, and Adam was very involved. Babies and dogs and dogs and cats and dogs and women at barbecues interacted with each other in hilarious combinations, and her son, who had no idea at all about Carla, laughed through his pasta at all the fun the people and animals were having. As she watched Adam watch, she was struck with a vague idea about the promise of life (as represented by the babies onscreen) and about not giving up on passions. While she looked at Adam, she understood that he was a baby with passions.

Jillian reflected on some of her youthful passions, and she was taken by a feeling of total integration. Not just the integration of her body and mind, but also a synthesis of that integrated self with the room, the atmosphere, and with the general chronology and flow of time and events, universally speaking. This was a feeling she sometimes got from motivational phrases, and she knew it to be the feeling of God. Whatever thought was in her mind when she got this feeling, she knew she owed it to God to follow.

"I'm not going to give up on my dream," she whispered. She had a flash as bright as reality—no, brighter—of walking the dog, and maybe the dog would be big enough for Adam to ride like a tiny pony, or maybe she could get out the stroller and the dog could pull Adam, but either way the dog and boy were happy and her hands were empty and flapping at her sides.

"Yes, I'll do it," she whispered.

So what about Carla? Carla was in the past.

"Hey, Adam," she said. "Which do you like better, doggies or kitties?"

"Doggies!" he said, but he said it like "d'ah-gaze," and lifted his arms above his head and made fists of his hands, which resulted in the knocking over of his dinner onto the floor.

Mommy scooped it back into his bowl and set it on the coffee table, thinking one day she'd yell, "The dog, the dog!" when food got knocked on the floor.

Adam was put to bed. Jillian got into her own bed and rearranged the bras and other dirty clothes that were mixed in with the covers so there'd be room for her to sit and, later, sleep comfortably. She looked until she found a website called Pups of Love, which was a rescue center for dogs who had been sexually abused—dogs who had belonged to pet-store breeders and had been pregnant their whole lives. Some of them were still puppies themselves. A one-year-old? Isn't that still a puppy? Some of these one-year-olds had birthed dozens of babies. She watched half a video and started sobbing. This is definitely it, she thought. And the adoption fee was a fraction of what the Humane Society wanted, so she'd have extra money for other things.

Jillian had a dream that night that she was riding an enormous dog through a meadow. The dog was running at full speed and its mouth was frothing. The breeze caught the froth from the dog's mouth and splattered her in the face with it. The froth ran across her cheeks and her hair, which was rippling wildly in the breeze, until it separated from her and the dog, hung in the air for a minute, then fell gently onto a patch of little yellow flowers. The meadow was endless and the dog's energy was endless and the sky had a few nice, white clouds.

That night, Megan had a dream that it was her birthday, and Randy took her to Chuck E. Cheese. They were in the arcade and Megan started to play a video game that was underneath a Skee-Ball table. The controller was a large, soft red ball that, when she squeezed it, activated little cartoon mice that really beat the shit out of each other. She sat under the Skee-Ball table for a very long time, rapidly squeezing the ball controller until the alarm buzzed and she had to get up, get in the shower, and take the bus to work.

The bus was the same as always, the elevator and the hallway were the same as always, the greeting from Jillian was the same as always, the way her desk felt was the same as always, the slowness of the computer was the same as always, and as always Megan's mind idly floated to the subject of suicide.

Halfway through the day, Megan started dicking around on the internet. She made her browser window as small as she could, paused for a second, and then looked up "Carrie Wilkins." She found Carrie's website, and on it, this bio:

Hi, my name's Carrie. I'm 26. I make things. I paint and I write, but mostly I design. I like to make things beautiful, or creative. I make my own food and I'm trying to grow my own beets. A lot of people around me seem unhappy and I don't understand why. I freelance because I know I'd go insane if I couldn't make my own schedule—I believe variety is the zest of life. I know I want a dog someday soon, and sometimes I make lunch at 3 a.m.

I believe in the power of collaboration, and I'd love to work with you!

What a total asshole. What does she have, some kind of a pact with Satan?

The picture next to Carrie's bio had some kind of heavy filter on it that made it look vintage, and she had a friendly but aloof look on her face. She was flanked on both sides by plants and was wearing an oxford shirt with fancy shorts and had a cool necklace. It was an outfit, for sure, like all of Carrie's clothes were outfits, which Megan always thought of as outdated or something only children did.

The website linked to a blog, which was mostly photos of Carrie doing different things. It didn't take too long to find the picture of her with the llama with a caption about how she and her boss got it from a homeless guy.

And then just products. Pictures and pictures of products, and then little captions about how the products inspired her.

Motherfucker, thought Megan. She doesn't get it at all. It

was like looking at an ad for deodorant or laundry soap that made you feel smelly and like you'd been doing something wrong that the person in the ad had already figured out, but since it was an ad, there was no real way to smell the person and judge for yourself whether or not the person stank, and that was what she hated, hated, hated most of all.

I make things, gee-wow. You think you're an artist? Do you really thing this *blog* is a representation of art, that great universalizer? That great transmigrator? This isolating schlock that makes me feel like I have to buy into you and your formula for happiness? *Work as a freelance designer, grow beets, travel, have lots of people who like you, and above all have funsies!*

"Everything okay?" asked Jillian.

"Yeah, what?"

"Breathing kind of heavy over there, just making sure you were okay and everything."

"Oh, uh-huh, I'm fine," said Megan.

"It's not . . . something I'm doing, is it?"

"What? No. No, I'm fine," said Megan.

How could someone not understand that other people could be unhappy? What kind of callous, horrible bullshit was that to say to a bunch of twenty-year-olds, particularly, when this was the time in life when things were even more acutely painful than they were in high school, that nightmare fuck, because now there were actual stakes and everyone was coming to grips with the fact that they're going to die and that life might be empty and unrewarding. Why even bring it up? Why even make it part of your mini-bio?

She copied and pasted Carrie's bio into an email to Randy and bolded the part about not understanding pain. The subject line was SEE? and the message was, "A little callous, don't you think?"

Randy had been about to email Carrie about helping with a new contract when he got the email.

"Hey, guess what?" said Jillian.

"Huh," said Megan. She'd closed the internet and was going to do some work and not think about things for the next few hours.

"I think I found a good place to get a dog."

"I thought you didn't have the money right now," said Megan.

"Weeelll," said Jillian. "But I really want one. I really feel like this is the right time in my life."

"Okay. I guess I just didn't get my first dog until I was in high school because my parents had to pay off their student loans first, so I think of your forties as the time to get a dog," said Megan.

Jillian looked at Megan like she hadn't heard. I can say anything, thought Megan, and only what she wants to go in goes in.

"Awww," said Jillian. "Well, it's this really cool place with rescue dogs on the outside of town. These aren't just dogs whose owners can't take them anymore, these are dogs who've experienced real trauma."

"Aren't those the kinds of dogs who need around-the-clock care and training?"

"Awww, but I think we can take care of one. I already

have it all figured out. With the extra money I get from the coding business I'm starting, I can hire a dog walker, and then when I go down to part-time hours, you know, to work from home more, I'll only need the walker two days a week."

Ah, yes, the coding business.

Sometimes Jillian could see what was to come with such clarity it was as if she were already paying the dog walker with a sealed white envelope of cash.

Sometimes Megan wanted to walk over to Jillian and block her airways.

As it was Friday, it was now time for serious drinking. On the walk home from the bus, Megan picked up a twelve-pack at a discounted price. Before taking her shoes and jacket off, she opened a can and finished half of it in the kitchen, standing by the door.

Jillian picked up Adam and drove home and, while they were eating dinner, asked him if he wanted to have a doggie. He looked at her earnestly and said, "Yes, I want to have a doggie."

Randy hadn't asked Carrie to help him with his project after all, even though it was something he really thought would be fun. While Megan was standing by the door, ravaging her can of beer, Randy received a text message.

"Oh. Do you want to go to Will's house?" asked Randy.

Megan took off her shoes. "Yeah, sure."

He came to hug her.

"Hold on, let me get my stuff off first."

She took off all her crap, handed him a beer, put the rest of the beers in the refrigerator, gave him a side hug and a kiss on the cheek, then walked to the living room and sat on the couch.

"Ah," she said. He sat in the chair by the couch. "How was your day, honey?" she asked.

"It was good," he said. "We got a new client who wants us to make a website for his barbershop."

"Cool." Megan nodded, maybe a second too long.

Jillian thought she should really clean up before the dog got here, but she needed to lie down first.

Megan emptied the rest of the beers into her purse and they walked over to Will's. "I feel like I've been waiting to get wasted all week," she announced.

"Hmm. The weather is nice," said Randy.

"Um, is it usually nice this time of year? I can't remember."

"Well, I think it's usually nice like this some days, and then not so nice other days," said Randy.

"Yeah, right."

Mercifully, there were people at Will's when they got there. Megan felt a little anxious, but she had a plan. She sat on the couch next to an ashtray and got a beer and a cigarette out of her bag. The beer distracted her from the inevitable Friday question, which was, "Hmm, what am I going to do for the next sixty-two hours now that it's the weekend?" Four beers calmed that pretty quickly, and the cigarettes helped her drink faster and more. If she started to get the spins, she could switch to cigarettes exclusively.

She knew all of her habits were painfully interesting.

It would be difficult to talk to anyone but Randy until the fourth beer, but if it had to happen, she could always smoke a cigarette and drink a *little* bit faster.

"I don't give a fuck, I don't *give* a fuck," was one of Megan's mantras. She finished her first party beer and started the second. She looked around at all the people in the living room. She didn't see Will. She kind of liked Will. She thought, "I don't give a *fuck*," while moving her head and shoulders back and forth a little.

She hadn't meant to move, but quickly reminded herself that she didn't give a fuck either way.

"What are you laughing at?" asked a guy who hit on her sometimes, for some reason.

"Myself, because I am an idiot."

"Cool."

"Yeah."

"Hey, can I have a cigarette?" he asked.

"Of course, why not, right?" she said.

"So, what's up?"

"Uh, nothing really at all."

"Oh, yeah? I find that hard to believe."

"Well, I work at a gastroenterologists' office as a medical

records technician, which means I look at saltine-sized photos of diseased anuses and colons all day. And I don't really have that much free time, but the free time I do have I spend trying to get drunk enough to forget my miseries," said Megan, holding her beer can up to the guy for a cheers.

He looked at her sideways, then gave her the cheers.

"Well, at least it's a funny job. Is it interesting? Are you into computers?" He was a smooth young man.

"No, I'm not really that into computers. And, also, our computers are always broken, so if I were into them, this job would be even more frustrating."

"Oh. Okay. Well, how did you get the job? Are you interested in medicine?"

"Oh, god no, not at all. I'm kind of a hypochondriac. If I see a malady, I absorb it. So I don't think I'd ever want to," she searched for the words, "advance in this field."

"Oh, okay."

Megan shifted. "I got this job through my primary doctor. I came in to see him about migraines and minor panic attacks, and he told me that occupation was good medicine and that the doctor down the hall was hiring. I hadn't had a job in ten months and I was living off my parents. It was making me cry every day."

"Oh."

Megan opened her third beer and flipped open the top of her box of cigarettes. She rolled the cigarette around between her fingers before lighting it. She thought it might be soothing. A girl walked up to them and punched Megan's new boyfriend in the arm.

"Hey, James, what's up, man?" said the girl.

She seemed like a happy young person. They ought to just, you know, go to the other side of the living room together, this girl and James.

"Oh, I got you one of those roadkill pelts I was telling you about," said the new girl. "They're actually a lot more beautiful and a lot less gross than I thought they'd be."

Oh my god, everyone in this world is just way too interested in things, thought Megan.

"Hey, do you want to sit here?" Megan asked.

"You don't mind?"

The girl asked this as if Megan had just done her a great kindness.

"Oh, um, no. Not at all. Just let me get my bag," said Megan.

"Hey, Megan, do you know Sarah?" asked James.

"No, I don't think we've met," said Megan, holding out her hand.

Sarah shook it.

"I've seen you a lot, though," said Sarah.

"Yeah, well, that's natural," said Megan. "Bye, guys."

A tiny-feeling hand pinched Megan's elbow.

It was Amanda!

"Hey, Megan," said Amanda.

"Hey, you want to go outside with me?" Megan asked. "I was just going to smoke."

"Oh, I think you can smoke inside," said Amanda.

"Yeah," said Megan. "I know. But I want to go outside."

"Oh, um," said Amanda. She looked around and then said, "Okay, sure."

"Ppphhhbbbffff," said Megan, leaning against the back porch railing. "What the fuck."

"What?" said Amanda.

"Eh, nothing. I feel weird today."

"I'm sorry."

"Why?" asked Megan.

"Oh, I mean, it's sympathy, not an apology."

"I know," said Megan, lighting a cigarette.

She offered one to Amanda, who waved her hand "No" at it.

"If I don't quit smoking, I'm going to kill myself," said Megan.

"Are they starting to take their toll?"

"No, I mean I'm going to deliberately commit suicide if I can't do something as simple as not slowly poisoning myself."

"Eh, you're young. The right time to quit will present itself," said Amanda.

"Do you really believe that? Do you really think there'll be some day when I feel capable enough to resist the nicotine addiction? And be able to unburden myself of the glamorous and romantic associations I have with smoking? You really think that's going to happen?"

"Well, yeah. All things we do but don't completely like are phases. Sometimes they're long-standing phases, but, I mean, they're phases. I remember wetting the bed until first grade and just really wondering when it would stop, and feeling the same way you do when my parents told me I'd grow out of it. I really thought it would never stop."

"What, are you a serial killer or something?"

"No. What kind of a thing is that to say?"

"Serial killers wet the bed, that's all."

"Lots of people wet the bed until they're seven. Six and seven, that's still a baby, I think. I'm just trying to relate our experiences."

"Yeah, okay."

They listened to the sound of other people's chatter. The porch was half full with people.

"I wet the bed, too," said Megan. "Until first grade. It's no big deal."

"I know it's no big deal, that's why I used it as an example."

"But it's different, because it's not like I learned how to wet the bed and then got addicted to it even though it was starting to kill me. It's not like bed-wetting was all the rage but the pee was, like, transdermally poisoning me."

"I guess that's one difference. Still, you should give it a few more years before committing suicide. Things might change."

"Yeah, I guess I was just being kind of dramatic," said Megan.

"Oh really?" said Amanda.

Megan sighed and opened another beer.

They hung out and drank, and at some point someone started smoking weed out there on the porch. Megan was drunk enough to think she wanted some. She eyed the people who were smoking. They all looked like they were pretty close friends and like they were having a real conversation. They were laughing and saying "Nuh-uh" and stuff like that.

"I want to smoke some of that weed," said Megan.

"Then ask for some."

Megan winced. "You do it?"

Amanda rolled her eyes. "Hey," she said to the group in general. "Can we trade you guys beer or smokes for a few hits of that?"

"Whatever, just have some," said one of the guys.

"Cool," said Amanda.

"Thanks," said Megan.

The pipe had a bug-eyed glass crocodile on it. Megan drunkenly identified with it for its mute and endless proximity to all this social fun. She felt like a warty little toad or a troll or a guy who was so visibly lonely that everyone thought he might start beating off or crying just for the feeling of connection he would get from all that wild, concentrated attention. She raised the pipe, tried to look the croc in the eyes, took a massive undergrad hit, and then re-inhaled it through her nose. A "French" inhale. She raised her eyebrows in gratitude in the general direction of the pot smokers.

Amanda took a small sip off the pipe and passed it back and, in a surprisingly genuine tone, said, "Thanks."

"I feel like a fucking freak," said Megan.

"Well, you're not a freak," said Amanda.

"Oh, god, yes I am."

"No you're not."

As the weed worked its way through Megan's system, she became more and more pantheistic. She became a living symbol for her emotions and, in response to the honor, her emotions began to swell. As they swelled, she felt simultaneously less stable and more happy, but happy in an awful way, since her happiness had something vaguely to do with death and complacency. No, not complacency. Acceptance, maybe? No, complacency.

She looked at all the people on the porch and only sort of heard Amanda say, "You're just a normal person who hates her job, but you've got a lot of nice things going for you. You're in a stable *relationship*, for one thing, which is something I wouldn't mind having. You know, I have pains in my life, too, but I manage. You manage, too. You're not a freak, and you don't turn people off except when you pout all the time, which you're doing now, but, geez, you're fine, all right? Stop being so overly self-involved. You have support from family and friends and everything is generally okay. Okay?" Which was a funny backdrop to the exalted feeling she was having of being one with the moment, being one with the porch in its misery, reveling in and revering this capsule of synthesized misery.

"I'm not trying to kiss your ass or anything, I'm trying to get you to snap out of it, because it's not a great way to relate to people. You're not a freak. Are you even listening to anything I'm saying? You're not even looking at me and I'm trying to help you."

I guess she gets pissed when she's high, thought Megan.

"The thing I have going for me," said Megan, "is that I don't even have to be here if I don't want to be." When she said "here" she pointed her finger down at the porch and held her hand in that position for a little too long, and she and Amanda made eye contact, which Amanda thought was aggravating, but which Megan thought was intense and transcendent.

"You're not even listening at all," said Amanda.

"Oh, I hear you, but I don't agree with you that having a boyfriend and having a mom and dad are, like, some kind of prime jewels in life. Because I know what my prime jewels are," why was she saying that—prime jewels? "and they are the moments in which all of those things—those baser things—melt into the background and I can feel like I know something that other people don't know and I can go other places if I need to and explore other feelings of meaning and stuff."

Megan kept talking. The way she thought she sounded was not the way she really sounded. Amanda stopped listening, because she could feel herself becoming offended in an impassioned way. The way Amanda saw it—kind of her one strong philosophy in life—was that it was impossible to "explore the complications of human feeling," as Megan was calling it, while you felt miserable. Those explorations were best left for times of reflection, when your judgment was not confused by the horrible lens of self-hatred. She knew this was not an original idea, but it didn't need to be. The way she understood Megan was that Megan's preoccupation *was* with these "baser" things—having stability, having a decent job, having health, having a group of people to support her. Amanda based this understanding on Megan's monomaniacal preoccupation with "that asshole and her stupid fucking job," "that asshole and his successful project," "those assholes and their stupid clique," "those fuckers and their homemade Tupperwares of kale." If you see something you're envious of—really genuinely envious of, not just that you admire—the only escape hatch from that feeling is to insult the object, to tart it up like an idiot, and then parade it around as something ridiculous, but that was a hatch that just led to a deeper and more confusing layer of self-doubt and self-dislike. It was obvious and sad to Amanda, but not sad enough. Megan wasn't paying her to listen to this. Amanda's week had been hard, too, and she was just trying to relax with some friends, but since she was the only one who seemed to have any tolerance for Megan, Megan clung to her. And she knew that Megan thought insulting things about her, too, and that was the thing that fired her up.

"People think happiness is some kind of sign of complexity, but it's not," said Megan.

"Oh, do they?" said Amanda. "I always thought people mistook brooding as a sign of complexity."

Megan gave her an I Dare You look.

"You must think I'm an idiot," said Amanda.

Megan continued the look.

"Let me call your bluff and say this," said Amanda. "There's no one on this planet, not even my mother, who I like enough to stand around and soak up this selfish, whiny-baby bullshit from. A week? Okay, everyone has their weeks, but honestly I don't even remember why we're friends. This is miserable. I don't know what I'm doing out here with you. There are people here who I don't even know who I'd rather talk to than you right now. You seem to think you're doing me a favor by hanging out with me. I find that laughable. I'd rather hang out with that guy," she pointed to a white-faced, slump-eyed guy in a beanie, "who looks like he might barf in my face, than hang out with you for another second. I don't know how much more clear I can be. I was just trying to give you a pep talk and you started shitting all over me. You are unbelievably draining, you self-serving, shallow, talentless waste of time."

Megan's I Dare You face had become stuck, but not without absorbing some of the psychotic torture that was going on behind it. It was a damn silly position to be in, trying to hold the bluff when it had already been called.

"I'm going to go inside now," said Amanda.

The potheads weren't eavesdropping as covertly as they might have liked. Amanda left.

"I think I'm going to go into the yard," said Megan, to no one. "Good evening," she said to the pale-faced guy in the beanie.

Her legs felt crazy and her hands were clammy.

"This is awful," she said. She said it in a kind of hollow, matter-of-fact way.

It was difficult to walk down the stairs. Her purse of beer was tipping her to the side.

"This is terrible."

She crawled under the porch and sat by the air conditioner and looked out into the yard. She could hear the people on the porch talking, not about her, just talking about whatever they wanted to. They weren't really that interested.

Spring nights were so fucking nice.

That elevated feeling she'd had earlier while she was shit talking all of human behavior came back, and as it came back she started laughing a horrified laugh, because that swelling feeling was exactly the same feeling she always had before she started sobbing. She hadn't recognized it ten minutes ago, but that was why the feeling had been so familiar. Not because her consciousness was tapping into the ineffable, but because she was about to cry and had cried before. She sat there with her eyes wide and her mouth open, laughing noiselessly. Then she started crying, which only made her laugh more.

Her body felt like nothing, not dense like it usually did.

I could stay here like this forever, she thought. This is infinity's moment.

"Ha ha ha, uugh."

Infinity's moment sounded like the jargon of a pedophile, and the phrase repulsed Megan, but she couldn't stop thinking it. "Would you like to go to the Movie Star Room, Tracy?" Like "infinity's moment" would be what the pedophile called his orgasm.

Several feet above and behind Megan, Amanda walked up to Randy.

"Can I talk to you?" she said.

"Sure, what's up?"

"I'm really sorry, I feel like kind of an asshole."

"What's up?" said Randy.

"Megan and I got into a fight, and I think I might have really hurt her feelings. I feel like an asshole."

"Are you okay?"

"Yeah, I'm fine, but I don't really want to . . . I'm sorry to say this, but I don't really think I can talk to her right now, but I think she might be under the porch crying. I'm sorry, I know this is shitty."

"Uh, really, Amanda, this isn't your fault. She's been kind of nasty lately. I'm sorry."

"Hey, she's not your responsibility."

Randy wince-smiled.

Back under the porch, Megan was grinning and crying. Oh my god, someone's coming down here, she thought. But this is infinity's moment, don't they know that? Ha ha ha, go away, go away, go away. Don't you know this is a special moment and that I can't talk right now, not even to tell you to go away, so just go away, go away?

She looks scary, thought Randy. Why is she smiling like that?

If I don't look at them? She stared ahead. Please go away, you know I don't really like social situations, ha ha ha. You know I don't do well in social situations, ha ha ha.

She's just really drunk.

Oh, it's Randy, my poor little Randy!

Randy scooted down next to her and said, "Hey, baby. Amanda told me you two got in a fight."

"Uuuoooohhhhh," said Megan. "Uuuuuhoohh."

He covered her with his torso and put his arms around her.

"My poor mama hen, my poor Randy."

"What?" said Randy. "I can't hear you."

"My poor mama hen."

"I can't—"

"I'm sorry, I'm sorry."

God, what a relief to just be able to cry like a normal person, without smiling. What a fucking relief.

"Honey, what's going on with you?"

Megan sobbed and said "sorry" while she thought thank you, thank you, oh, thank you.

He pulled away slightly and her arms tightened around him. She imagined being a python and coiling around him so she could kill him and eat him and keep him with her all the time.

"I'm going to go inside and get our stuff and say good night to some people, okay?"

Megan nodded. Randy left. Megan thought about Randy saying goodbye to some people while he gathered their stuff, and she cringed.

"I have a few more minutes left," she whispered. "A few more minutes in infinity's moment, ha ha ha ha. Oh, fuck, I'm such an idiot, that's so gross, I'm a disgusting piece of shit."

He came back down the stairs and crawled down to meet her.

"Here you go, sweetie." Her handed her some tissues, which she used to blow her nose and wipe the gooey tear bullshit off her face.

"Drink this."

She drank a sip of the glass of water.

"The whole thing, it's good for you."

She frowned at him, but then drank it.

"Where are you going to put it all?"

He took her tissues and put them in his pocket, then put the cup on the stairs.

The next day was a bad one.

The morning shower went something like this: Oh my god, I just don't want to be wrong about everything I've ever thought or to feel like I'm in some kind of dysfunctional state because of my personality, because if my personality is toxic, what am I supposed to do? Hey, what am I supposed to do about anything? I don't have anything at all in my life, I don't have anything that's only mine except this feeling, which isn't even something that's only mine or something to be proud of but, uuhhhhh, oh my god, what am I doing, there's nothing I can do, I'm just going to keep working at worse and worse jobs and I'm going to get sicker and sicker, my hair is going to fall out and my skin is going to get shitty, why am I even thinking about that right now, but I have to because it's just what I'm thinking, it's not like I'm making myself think this, it's just what I'm thinking. Oh god, oh god, oh my god.

All this was thought while sobbing silently and not washing, except for a little bit every few minutes because she had to (she was showering, after all) and then feeling totally ridiculous sudsing her buttcrack with the teal plastic bath poof while crying and thinking about the future. The horrible, empty future.

When she wasn't hiding around the apartment crying, she sat on the couch and felt physically hollow. Like she was resigned, but she didn't know to what. Randy was being careful around her in a way that really stung, but maybe she was imagining it and he wasn't acting differently. But if he wasn't acting differently after her display last night, wasn't that bad, too? She got back into bed and he sat at his computer quietly.

"Honey?" she said. He didn't hear her, but she didn't want to say it any louder, so she just said, "Honey," over and over again in the same quiet voice until he said, "Yeah?" and walked into the bedroom.

"I was calling you," she said.

"I didn't hear you," he said. "What's up?"

"I'm sorry," she said. "I feel really bad today."

He took her hand and she started crying, but a little cry, not those freaky silent sobs.

"What can I do? I don't know what to do," he said.

"I don't know what to do, either, I just don't know what to do with my life. I have no idea what to do and I feel so awful for putting you through this. I don't know what's wrong with me," and as she continued to apologize, her phone buzzed on the nightstand.

They both looked at it.

"Who is it?"

"Oh my god."

"Who is it?

"Oh my god."

She handed it to him.

It was a text message. It read "heres the cutie her name is crispy adams choice lol," and there was a picture of a Labrador attached to the text.

6

Jillian's Saturday had been way different. She called Pups of Love at eight in the morning and the woman on the line was a lot nicer than the woman from the Humane Society. This new woman said they had tons of young dogs as well as puppies, too, who needed a home so badly that the price of adoption couldn't be very high.

"I want one of the mothers," said Jillian.

"Then you're in luck," said the woman.

Jillian and Adam ate breakfast in the car on the way to the rescue place. They got it at the Starbucks drive-through. Jillian got her favorite kind of Starbucks and a scone and Adam got a donut and cocoa. They listened to and sang along with one of Adam's favorite albums for the first hour of the drive, then switched to one of Jillian's. She sang along to it while Adam said he had to pee. So far away, she thought, and tried to visualize herself NOT getting pulled over, ha ha, because that would not be a very good thing.

They drove until they came to the address, a ranch house with a big front yard. The gravel sounded under Jillian's tires and she felt like a TV detective pulling up to the scene. Adam thrashed in his seat and Jillian smiled at him while she unbuckled him.

What are you thinking about? she wondered. Oh, well.

A woman opened the front door of the house and said, "Are you here for the dogs?"

"Yeah, hi. I think we talked on the phone."

"You probably talked to our offices. I didn't talk to anyone on the phone."

"Okay," said Jillian, but the woman was smiling so it was fine.

"There are so many dogs in this area that we all take turns fostering some of them. Come on in."

"Oh, cool," said Jillian. "I'd love to do something like this."

She looked around the woman's living room. It was carpeted and there were nice framed posters on the walls. The cream-colored leather couches were covered with blankets, and two dogs on the floor chewed rawhide bones.

The woman rolled her eyes and said, "Those things get so nasty."

Jillian laughed and looked closer. The bones were dry and dirty on the bottoms, probably from the dogs' paws, which held them pinned to the floor, and as she looked farther up the shafts of the toys she saw that the material became a lighter off-white color and then even farther up it was soft and foamy. The dogs worked the bones in semicircles with their teeth, and a little bit of foam made of hide and spit dribbled from the dogs' lips. The dogs didn't look up at Jillian when she came near, they just gnawed their bones, breathing heavily, and making a rhythmic grinding sound.

"They're so calm," said Jillian.

"These are mine, Misty and Fancy Pants. See her pants?" The dog had darker fur on her hind legs that did look like pants. "They're used to company. I'm Emily." The woman held out her hand.

"I'm Jillian and this is Adam."

Jillian was embarrassed because her hands were sweaty, she was so excited, but she had to shake this woman's hand. If I pretend it's not sweaty, then it won't seem so sweaty, she thought.

Adam said hello but his attention was on the TV and the collection of movies underneath it. He imagined the woman might invite him to watch one and give him a sandwich, because most women wanted to do things like that for him.

"Let's go out to the run," said Emily.

Jillian's heart was pounding, she couldn't calm down. Who is this woman, what am I doing here? Okay, calm down, you know, it'll be great.

The back door was off the kitchen. Jillian could see it from the living room because there was an open wall above one of the kitchen counters. They walked through the kitchen, which had several bowls of dog food and water on the floor on children's place mats. The lower cabinets were held shut by rubber bands wrapped around the knobs. There was a loaf of bread on the counter. Emily opened the back door, turned and smiled at them, and said, "This way."

The backyard was nice and big and there were a few trees and a fence around the perimeter. It took a second to see where the dogs were. I guess this is what their natural camouflage is like, thought Jillian, noticing how the chocolate Labs blended into the shaded dirt under the trees and how the yellow Labs blended into the wood on the fence. A few white-and-brown-spotted dogs, which Jillian thought looked like English hunting dogs, walked around with toys in their mouths. "Oh, those look like Fancy Pants," she said.

"Yeah," said Emily. "Which one do you want to meet?"

"Adam?"

"I like those," said Adam. He pointed to the brown Labs under the tree.

"I guess we want to meet those chocolate Labs," said Jillian. Emily led them back to the tree and explained that, at least during the good weather seasons, it was better for the dogs to stay in a house with a yard.

"You know, better for them mentally. My house doesn't always look like this. I usually have nice hostas along that fence," she said, pointing to a dug-up spot along the fence.

"This is a really great thing you do," said Jillian.

Adam crouched in the shade by the Labs, who were initially indifferent to him.

"They don't bite, do they?"

"Not as far as I know. I think they're pretty kid-friendly."

"Hi, Choco," said Adam. Choco raised her head. Adam crouch-walked closer to the dogs while the women talked about the rescue center.

"You're Choco and you're Crispy. Hi, Crispy. Hi, Choco

the dog," he said. Crispy got up, wagged her tail, and walked up to Adam and began to sniff his crotch. "Hi, Crispy," he whispered.

"That dog's name is Peanut," Emily corrected. Adam didn't pay attention to her. "I named all the dogs," she said to Jillian. "That dog responds well to Peanut. It's best to pick two-syllable names."

Crispy licked the donut sugar off of Adam's hands. Jillian gave Emily the money order, and then Jillian, Adam, and Crispy loaded themselves into the car.

"Hey, maybe we can talk about other names," said Jillian.

"Why?" said Adam.

"Choco's a cute name, what about Choco?"

"But, the other one was Choco," said Adam. "This is Crispy."

He was so delightful and strange. Her hands were still sweaty, maybe even sweatier. She'd made sure she had enough cash to pick up dog food and a dog bowl and a leash at the Petco. The dog started trembling. Adam unbuckled his harness and leaned way over, embracing the dog and whispering, "Crispy, Crispy," and Crispy began to hyperventilate.

"Where are your collars and leashes?" asked Jillian. She was bent over, holding Crispy by the shoulders, and waddling toward the cashier.

"Right there," said the cashier, pointing to them. Jillian put her arms around the dog while Adam picked out a neon-green collar and a red nylon puppy leash that was maybe a little too short. Jillian attached these items to the dog and stood up. She stretched her back and Crispy shook her skin. They walked to the dog food aisle and picked out the food, two plastic bowls, and a fifteen-inch rawhide bone.

"This is our first dog," said Jillian to the cashier. She looked around and half picked Crispy up. "Can you just ring up these things while they're on her?"

"Can you just rip the tags off and hand them to me?"

"Oh, yeah, duh," said Jillian. She ripped the tags off and the cashier beeped them onto her total. Everything was a little over a hundred dollars. It was more than the adoption fee, but fuck it.

"Okay, okay," said Jillian in the car.

She walked the dog up the stairs to her apartment. "Welcome home, Crispy." Crispy walked around the apartment and sniffed things and looked generally confused. Every minute or so she would stop and jump backward, take a few steps sideways, look around, and then continue sniffing.

Jillian turned on the TV and gave Adam the remote. "Just let her sniff around a second, but let me know if she starts squatting."

The house wasn't picked up yet.

Jillian opened the kitchen window and walked around the house opening up the blinds. She set the Petco bags on the kitchen counter, got some scissors, cut off the little plastic loops from where the price tag had been, and hung the leash over the kitchen door. She walked around the apartment picking up dishes, then she picked up stray clothing and put it in the hamper in the bathroom. She moved the damp towels from the floor to the hamper. She wiped the crumbs off the kitchen counters and the kitchen table and put the fistfuls of crud in the trash can under the sink. She felt like she had to do this quickly, and she pivoted several times while she was holding the crud. Then she swept crud off the coffee table and side tables, then she went around picking up little wrappers and pieces of paper. She used a squirt bottle of all-purpose cleaner to dampen the counters and table, coffee table, and side tables. She glanced at Crispy, who was sitting underneath the living room's dining table.

We'll eat there tonight.

Then she got paper towels and went around the apartment, wiping in the order she'd sprayed. It took nine paper towels, more because of how much cleaner she'd used than how much dust and crud was on the surfaces. It hadn't been that messy.

She took the scrubber-sponge and scrubbed the stove and microwave, then she got the vacuum out of the pantry, emptied the canister into the trash can, and went around and did the living room and the kitchen. The bathroom and bedrooms would have to wait for a bit. First things first. The noise of the vacuum made Crispy get up and walk around in that sideways way she'd used earlier. Jillian looked at Crispy and thought, She'll get used to it. Maybe she'll even think the vacuum is funny later. Jillian put the vacuum back in the pantry after re-wrapping the cord, then looked around and thought.

The dishes.

She went to the sink and prewashed the dishes and loaded a full load into the washer, poured in the Cascade, and started it. The smell of warm, soapy water and damp, old food filled the kitchen. It mixed nicely with the smell of burnt rubber and dust, but the smell of cleaner was too strong. She opened more windows and lit the candles.

She got the dog bowls out of the shopping bag, then went to one of the kitchen drawers and got out a place mat. She put the place mat down on the ground next to the kitchen table, opened the bag of dog food, and then took a minute to carefully pour out a portion from the twenty-five-pound bag into the bowl on the table. She put the bag in the pantry next to the vacuum cleaner and looked at it. She got a chip clip and closed the open dog food bag, then shut the pantry door and filled the second bowl with water. When she set the bowls on the place mat they didn't fit. The bowls were too big. She would have to buy a bigger place mat.

She kept cleaning and cleaning and cleaning, running around back and forth between rooms and pivoting. She called this "getting into the rhythm."

The dog would need to pee soon. She gave the dog the rawhide bone.

She put her hands on her body and thought, I need to do the laundry, or no one will have clean underwear.

Crispy sat in the corner looking at the rawhide bone and Adam was watching commercials.

Jillian had to pee.

The sweet smell of the outside, the vacuum and the candles, the sound of the commercials and the dishwasher and some cars outside, her kid and Crispy in the same room with her, it was awful not to quite have these things yet. This would be perfect in a second, but there were still things to get in order.

She peed. The bathroom was covered in that layer of lint and hair that gets stuck in the steamed-in soap film. She'd clean that, too.

"Get your shoes on, we need to take Crispy out."

Crispy skidded away from the leash and was difficult to get down the stairs. She kept sitting down on the walk and Jillian kept thinking she'd get used to it, right?

"We need to talk to her to make her more comfortable."

They both started saying "good dog" over and over and Adam went up to trees and lifted his leg to mime peeing.

"Pee-pee pee-pee, ha ha ha."

Eventually, Crispy took a dump on the median. Jillian had forgotten to bring poop bags, so she looked around. She saw no one. "Come on," she said and they walked a little faster. She needed to tire them both out so they'd go to sleep so she could work and then, when everything was in place, she could wake them up and they could all cuddle on the couch like she'd been hoping they would. She skipped and galloped to get her kid and the dog to romp. Crispy seemed happy, and even romped a little and wagged her tail in short, weird bursts. Jillian smiled at them both. They walked for twenty minutes, until Jillian's feet were sore and Adam said he had to pee and Crispy started looking anxious.

When they got back, Jillian straightened out the pillows and blankets on the couch and turned on the TV. She tucked Adam into a little nest and gave him the remote.

"Take a little nap if you need to, I have to do the laundry."

She put some peanut butter on the rawhide and used it to
lure Crispy into the kitchen.

"Here's your water and food," she said, pointing to the
bowls on the place mat.

She dropped the bone by the bowls.

Her bedroom was dark. Even with the shades up, it didn't
get much light. She picked up her bras first and tossed them
into the bathtub, then picked up all the dirty clothes, separated out some things that still seemed clean, and took the rest
of the pile to the bathroom and dumped it on the floor. She
stripped the bed and laid the bottom sheet in the hallway. She
went to Adam's room, stripped his sheets, picked up his dirty
clothes and dumped them on the sheet. She put all of her
laundry from the floor and the hamper on the sheet pile, got
the soap and fabric softener, then bundled up the sheet—like
Santa, that was how she felt—and hauled it downstairs.

She didn't separate the colors, just separated the clothes
randomly into two machines and started them with extra
soap. The clothes smelled a little musky. Back upstairs she
opened her bedroom window and Adam's, put sheets on both
of their beds, made them up with the pillows and everything,
tucked a stuffed animal under the sheets on Adam's bed,
picked up his toys from the floor and put them in his bin. She
hung up the clothes she'd decided weren't dirty. She took the
bras from the tub and threw them into the hallway. She went
and got the cleaner and the paper towels and the kitchen
sponge and removed the film of hair and lint from the bathroom and polished the surfaces as well as she could. Then she
dried the bathroom a little with paper towels, filled the sink

with cold water and hand soap, and submerged her bras in it. She turned the fan on in the bathroom, threw away the paper towels, and dusted the surfaces in her room and Adam's, then she ran the vacuum again.

By then it was time to change the laundry.

She came back upstairs, rinsed her bras, and hung them over the shower rod. She watered the two dry-looking plants in the kitchen and put the hot, dull-smelling plates back into the cabinets. The sun was going down, and she didn't want to know where the dog was, not yet, not until everything was in place and she could enjoy it. She got an old blanket, folded it, and put it by the couch.

"That's Crispy's bed for now."

She got hair bands and used them to hold the cabinets closed, like in Emily's kitchen.

There was no juice in the refrigerator. She needed to go shopping.

She sat down next to Adam and they both called, "Crispy," and Crispy walked up to them slowly, wagging her tail fast and slow at alternating speeds.

"Crispy!"

Wag . . . wag . . . wagwagwag.

"Good dog, come here, Crispy!"

They all played for a minute, then Crispy sat on her bed. Jillian put away the laundry and made a grocery list, and when she looked over at Adam and Crispy watching TV together, she thought she was going to start crying, she was so close to being able to sit with them and relax.

"Will you be a good girl?" asked Jillian.

Crispy looked from side to side.

"We'll be right back, okay? Will you be a good girl?"

In the car, Jillian said, "We'll need to get her a crate for when I'm at work, and I think she needs some fetch toys, but we can use an old sock for now. Tie it in a knot. We can use peanut butter for treats, too, to save money for now."

Just talking out loud.

"What movie do you want to watch tonight, Adam?"

When they got back from the store, Jillian said, "One more thing before dinner and movies, okay?" and that's when she sent the photo message to Megan.

PART 2

1

That dog, that silly little dog (and, but, not that it was Crispy's fault) distracted her so much. The dog wasn't in the car, not physically, but, you know, Crispy's essence was in the car. The thought of Crispy, thinking about all the things Crispy needed. She was on the way to pick up a discounted crate from someone ten miles away, and the crate came with a pillow and it was in very good condition, according to the description online.

The crate would be forty, and she could go get bulk food at ALDI and not buy any lunch at the cafeteria and she could afford it. That's what she was thinking about when she ran the red light. It was yellow when her nose was over the crosswalk, wasn't that the law?

"Isn't that the law?" she argued.

"Ma'am, step out of the car," he said because she said she didn't have her license.

"Okay, but I'm sorry, it's the law isn't it?" Because she really did have her license, it was just that, you know.

Trembling, she handed it to him, hoping he wouldn't have some kind of machine that would get her in trouble. He raised his eyebrows and walked back to his car. Oh my god. The machine that would get her in trouble was surely in his car.

"Step out of the car please, ma'am."

"But I gave you my license. I don't have to get out of the car."

Why do they always fight it, these silly little mothers with their shit-filled cars and that frantic look in their eyes that made you—whether you were the type or not—want to smack them?

"Ma'am, I'm not asking," said the officer.

She exited the vehicle. The officer put his hand on his weapon, leaned back on his heel, and dared her, silently, to go ahead and try it, whatever it was.

"So, I don't see what the problem is. I'm just on my way home from work and I have to pick up my child. I was just going to get a crate for my new puppy." She said this like it was a threat. She looked at him like she hated him and needed him and that was the push he needed to detach. Floating free there, free from compassion, he smiled.

Why is he smiling? Her feelings, which were ricocheting, strengthened. They didn't define themselves, but they strengthened.

They always try to make you feel like you're getting in the way of them doing something more important, as if there's anything more important to an officer of the law than enforcing the law.

"Seems like you have some outstanding fines. Are you aware you're driving with a suspended license?"

"I told that woman that I was told I didn't have to pay."

"Turn around, ma'am."

"Excuse me?"

"Ma'am," he said, putting his hand on his piece again, oh god, he loved putting his hand on his piece. "Turn around and put your hands on the vehicle."

Jillian's stomach plummeted and things became slow. She saw people looking at her as they drove past. Her body relaxed and she did as she was told. The officer used his radio to say, "Bring a tow truck to Palatine and Quentin, we've got a car that needs to go to the impound."

Jillian was too angry to cry, was that why she wasn't crying?

"Oh, and bring some trash bags. Car's full of shit."

Ah, but then she started crying. The officer put his hand on her head and led her to the cop car and, still with his hand on her head (which covered over half of her skull), he made her duck into the backseat.

She was formally served and fined and her court date was mandatory and she had no car to get to work, so she didn't know what to do when she finally got home that night at 11:30 p.m. Elena from church group was sitting with Adam teaching him to color in between the lines, even though it was 11:30 p.m. and he already knew how.

"Why don't you go get ready for bed," said Elena. Adam hopped up and did as he was told, mostly because he was exhausted and wanted to go to bed and was sick of being bossed around about how to color, but his obedience to another woman's orders still hurt Jillian's feelings.

"Where's Crispy?" asked Jillian.

"In the bathroom, sleeping with the lights off," said Elena.

"Do you know where Jillian is?"

"No, do you?"

"No, I thought you might know."

"No, she didn't say anything."

"Was she here yesterday?"

"Yes."

"But not today?"

"No."

"Can you cover for her?"

"I have been. I mean, yeah, it's fine. Of course. Do you need anything?"

Dr. Billings shrugged.

Yesterday, Megan was still feeling demolished from the weekend and she and Jillian hadn't really talked, but Jillian had seemed normal. Her absence was intriguing.

Jillian was at home. She turned off her phone. When Elena showed up that morning to drop Adam off at day care, Jillian was dressed.

"Thank you so much for doing this for me."

"It's fine, what are friends for?"

"No, I mean, I really owe you one. Whenever you need something, if it's something I can do, you know, I'll do it."

Elena put her hand on Jillian's shoulder and said, "I know."

Jillian walked them to the door, said, "Just going to take the dog out once more before getting on the train," then went to the bathroom and looked at herself in the mirror. She started punching herself in the cheek and making a face like she was screaming. She stopped hitting herself, grabbed the edges of the sink, leaned forward, and started making a face like she was screaming even louder. She panted for a second and then took off all of her clothes and put on a nightgown.

The next day, Dr. Billings said, "Did you hear what happened to Jillian?"

"No," said Megan.

"She hit a deer with her car. Her car is totaled. She lives in the suburbs, you know. She called me this morning. She was at the doctor and trying to get her car fixed yesterday."

"Huh," said Megan.

"It's terrible," said Dr. Billings.

"Yeah, terrible," said Megan.

"Can you make her reminder calls?"

"Sure."

Later, Randy asked, "Why are you smirking like that?"

"I don't know," said Megan. She took off her jacket and bag and shoes, opened a beer, and said, "I don't know."

Randy sat at the table.

"I think the self-destruction that I predicted for Jillian is finally happening."

"Congratulations," said Randy.

Jillian wasn't sitting at her desk the next morning when Megan arrived, but Megan could sense her in the office. Megan could hear the other doctor, Dr. Schraeder, talking behind a partially closed door, and she could also hear Jillian saying "Yes ma'am" in a childish voice.

"Hi, Jillian," said Megan when Jillian came out into their desk area.

"Hey, Megan."

"How are you? Are you okay?"

"Yeah, you know, I just hit this enormous deer with my car," she said.

"Oh, no," said Megan.

They worked quietly. Dr. Billings came out and said, "Jillian! Good to see you again. How are you?"

"Oh, I'm still a little shaken up more than anything. But my back is killing me, too, and my car is, you know, absolutely useless. Umm . . ."

"Where were you driving that you came across a deer?" he asked. His question was innocent.

"Oh, I was picking up a dog from a rescue center outside of town."

Bold, thought Megan. A very bold choice.

"Ah, good. Was the dog hurt at all?"

"No, no one was hurt, we're all fine."

"Good, good. Well, good to have you back."

A truly needless fib. Megan sort of admired it.

Dr. Schraeder came out of the examination room. "Here you go, Jillian," she said, putting a piece of white paper on Jillian's desk.

"Thank you so much," said Jillian.

"Now that has two refills, and it's free of charge, okay? I'll cover it."

"Thank you so much." She breathed this, lower than a whisper.

When the doctors and patients had left for the day, Jillian said, "Hey, I'm sorry for leaving you all alone."

"It's okay."

"Yeah, everyone's being really nice about it. No one's mad and Dr. Schraeder just gave me a prescription for some thirty-milligram Tylenol T3s with codeine," she said. "You know, for the pain of my injuries."

"Oh, wow, I didn't even know she could prescribe that."

It was always interesting the way things worked out, thought Jillian on the ride home, the train taking her where she needed to go, chugging along, her thoughts free to roam. A bottle of midgrade painkillers in her purse. A kind of general hilarity all around her. She'd thought she might get fired or reprimanded and she'd been planning to settle into a comfortable depression, but no. They'd been really nice. And Megan hadn't said anything about the dog, and it tickled Jillian that Megan could be so understanding.

I was in a really bad car accident, she thought. She carried herself like someone who had been in a car accident. She rubbed her shoulder and drew a breath in through her teeth. She visualized the deer and how she hadn't screamed and how Adam had thought it was exciting. The dog barked at the deer to protect them all from the deer. The deer wasn't hurt, it ran away, just smashed up the car real bad, and now she had horrible back pain. She shook her head and exhaled.

If anyone asked, she'd tell them that's what happened. "Oh my gosh, that happened to me, too," they'd say.

Sunset on the train was great. It was only eighty dollars a month for the pass, maybe she could get Elena to pick up Adam all the time. This might have been the best thing that had ever happened to her, getting into this silly car accident.

She got home and let Crispy out of the bathroom. She'd pooped on the floor and chewed up the bath mat. Jillian picked up the bath mat and Crispy lunged at it. "Oooohhh, I forgot to leave you your bone, didn't I, you crazy girl?" she said, tugging the bath mat while Crispy bore down on the other end. "Time to go on out," she said.

Dinner was cooking when Elena came by to drop Adam off.

"Hey, you want to stay for dinner? I made plenty."

"No," said Elena. "I have to get home and make dinner for my own family."

"Oh, okay," Jillian said. "Well, anytime, you know. Thanks for picking him up."

They laughed at the movie while they ate dinner. It was great that the apartment was still kind of clean from the weekend. She changed her boy into his pajamas, tucked him in, and then went to the bathroom to get ready for bed. She slipped into a fresh nightgown and washed her face, something she didn't always do. She brushed and flossed. Then she went into the dark apartment and found her purse on the kitchen chair. Crispy walked up to her and looked at her.

"Hi, Crispy," she whispered.

She got the bottle of medicine just so she could put it away in the cabinet.

When she was back in the bathroom, she looked at the bottle and said, "I've been in a bad accident."

2

Things were still pretty awkward between Megan and Randy, and she hadn't heard anything from or said anything to Amanda since the fight. But did she still go to the grocery store and buy dinner and stuff? Oh, totally, yeah, of course, of course, because life just keeps grinding on, right?

That day she thought, Fuck it, and went to the smaller grocery store. The store was for rich people, but fuck it, right? There were delights there.

She wanted to make something out of vegetables. The selection was small but everything did look so much healthier. There were summer squash the size of a baby's arm and baby bok choy that looked clean and smooth and not like a bunch of slugs had been fucking and barfing on it in the back of a truck for weeks. So this is how the better half eats. She picked out two well-formed bunches of baby bok choy and put them in her basket. There was a wall of salad dressing in a refrigerated shelf that she stared at for five minutes. Next to that was a section for juices and anciently formulated teas with helpful bacteria. On one of the teas was a drawing of a thin female torso with a spiral on it that looked like a twister. Detoxification. Gotta get this inside me. It was five dollars. She picked up the bottle and stood in front of the case for two minutes, staring at it. It was a glass bottle. She needed a sweet potato. They were two dollars, but they didn't have those suspicious gray holes bored into them that she was used to coring out. That would be fun. Just wash it and bake it. That would be fun, yeah.

And something fun to eat. The snack aisle. Oh, yeah, I like this, she thought. Cruelty-free agave dino gummies, gluten-free-cookie mixes, puffed and naturally flavored corn and rice balls, crackers made mostly out of raw seeds, a bag of dried Himalayan goji berries. Yeah, cool.

Ultimately these things were too expensive, so she picked a small-farm cheese and a six-pack of nice beer. "I mean, I work all the time. This is why I work, isn't it?" she mumbled. "I'm a hard worker. I can buy this cheese. It's just cheese, I guess." She was standing by the cheese case, holding the cheese, looking at the cheese, and pumping herself up to buy it. "Fuck it," she mumbled, and tossed it in her basket.

When she got home, Randy asked, "Oh, cool, what's the occasion?"

"I dunno," said Megan. "I just wanted to get us some fancy groceries."

Randy poked through the bag. "No snacks?" he said.

"The snacks were all stupid," said Megan. "It was all, like, tiny bags of dried Himalayan berries for nine bucks."

"Hey, nice cheese."

"And I got some fancy beer."

"Can I have one?" he asked.

"Obviously," said Megan. "And look at how nice that bok choy looks."

"Oh, yeah," said Randy. He wasn't looking at it closely enough. He was looking for snacks. "Do we have any bread for this cheese?" he asked.

"God fucking damn it."

"What?"

"No, we don't have any fucking bread for that cheese."

"Oh, it's okay, baby."

"Well, what's the point of the cheese if you can't eat it?"

"We could put it on the potato. Hey, don't look at me like that."

"We're not going to put the cheese on the fucking potato," said Megan. "That's stupid."

"Well, hold on," said Randy. In the cabinet he found some stale tortilla chips. "Here. We can eat it with these."

"Are those even good?"

"They're probably fine," said Randy.

Megan baked the potato and cooked the greens with hot pepper. They ate the nine-dollar cheese on the stale tortilla chips and Megan said, "Well, I guess this nine-dollar cheese is pretty good."

"Oh, come on, it's great."

"It would be great if we didn't have to eat it with these shitty chips."

Randy sighed. "Do you remember Kelly?"

"Uuuh, sort of," said Megan.

"She's opening up a vintage clothing store in the neighborhood."

"Wow."

"And," said Randy, looking at her sideways, "I'm doing the website for it." He wiped his mouth and took a sip of beer.

"Oh, cool. What's it going to, uh, look like?"

"I don't know, I haven't started it yet. But she's having a launch barbecue thing in two weekends, so that's my deadline. She's going to give out business cards and coupons and stuff. It's going to be a pretty big thing."

"Sounds fun," said Megan. Sounds like my fucking nightmare.

"So, you want to go? She's paying me."

"Paying you to go to her party?"

"No, Megan, paying me to do the website."

"Oh, that's cool."

3

You know that part in *The Little Mermaid* when Ariel has just seen Eric for the first time and she's swimming around the dressing room, combing her hair and singing? And all her sisters are like, "Whoa, she's happy"?

Jillian was on the train monologizing to herself.

When she got off, she sighed and noted that the sidewalk had never looked so beautiful. She reached up and touched the buds on the trees and smiled and hummed. She even did a little twirl half a block from the office building.

It was okay that she was late. Megan was always late, so it was okay for her to be late once, geez.

"Oh, hey, Miss Megan," she said. Megan looked at her quickly, then looked back at her computer.

"Hi, Jillian."

Jillian sighed, put her purse up on the coatrack, and plopped herself down in the chair, spinning around in it slightly. "So, what's new?" she asked.

"Nothing," said Megan.

"Hmmm," said Jillian. "Geez, I did not get much sleep last night."

"Oh yeah?"

"Too much caffeine too late," she giggled to herself.

"Yeah, you're not supposed to have caffeine at night."

"Oh, but it's okay because I'm in such a great mood."

"So you're feeling better? From your accident?"

"Oh, you know, I'm still pretty sore from it and my car is still totaled."

"Yeah, but you're feeling better?"

"Hmm, nope." Jillian laughed. "You know, it takes longer than two days to recover from an accident."

"Uh-huh," said Megan.

"I wonder if I can get a massage covered by my insurance."

You'd probably have to've had an actual injury to get that, thought Megan.

"Oh, yeah, that'd feel real nice," said Jillian. "Do you want to get some cookies for lunch? Just have only cookies for lunch?"

Megan wanted to scream.

Jillian almost snort-laughed when she said this, oh man it was like a truth serum or something. The one pill last night had just made her feel wired and made her sore back feel better, but this morning when she'd taken three, it was like a truth serum. Being on truth serum was fun.

"No, not really," said Megan. "I brought a salad."

"Oh, you and your salads," said Jillian. "I know I'm going

to have cookies at some point today, I just know I am, so I thought I'd offer to share some cookies with you."

I can afford my own cookies, thought Megan. "Uh, no, I'm cool. I don't really like to eat cookies that often."

"Really?" said Jillian. "I thought all people liked eating cookies. But I guess you're above cookies. You're, like, able to resist the temptation."

"It's not even really a temptation to have cookies for lunch," said Megan.

"Are you sure I couldn't tempt you to have one or two cookies with your salad?"

"No, really, I'm fine," said Megan.

"Do you think they deliver cookies?"

"What? Who? Who is they?"

"Oh, you know, the place we get our food from sometimes."

"I don't know. Would it really be worth it? Do you really want to tip and pay a delivery fee just for a couple of cookies? Not to mention the waste of gas."

Oh, I'm not going to just get a couple of cookies, thought Jillian and almost laughed that exploding snort laugh again.

"Hmm, I guess you're right," said Jillian.

There was silence for a minute.

When the minute was up, Jillian said, "Can you, um, answer calls for me while I'm gone? I'm going to run out to the Walgreens real quick."

"Yeah, sure," said Megan. Jillian left with her purse and Megan sat in her chair with a "What the fuck?" face.

As soon as she shut the door, Jillian let the laugh out and

doubled over a little bit, then straightened out and sighed. "I didn't really need to bend over like that," she said to the empty hallway. "Just felt like it."

"Did you know that Walgreens has home-baked cookies?" Jillian said in the grocery aisle at the Walgreens. "Incredible."

I want to make sure I'm fully stocked, she thought. She thumbed through the cookies, which were the size of compact discs and individually wrapped in cellophane. Peanut butter, peanut butter M&M, sugar M&M, oatmeal raisin, chocolate nut. Guess I should get one of each. But maybe two chocolate nut. There came that old laugh again, because it was she who was the real nut. She looked to the side. Good that no one was there.

But maybe she needed something else. Oh my god, Pop-Tarts were on sale. Those would make a good lunch. Something salty. Hey, these nuts are smoked. That sounds like a health nut thing. Megan was such a health nut! Then that damn laugh again. Two Paydays, because they were on sale, and then a bottle of water. Yeah, today seemed like a water day. Evian. Oh, cool, they have little Crystal Lights right in the water fridge. Cool. Jillian took her armload up to the cashier and felt that laugh bubbling up in her chest again. And it felt good to suppress, too, that was how fun the laugh was.

She bent over the counter and slowly unfolded her arms, letting the snacks tumble out in front of the cashier. "Didn't want to drop any of it," said Jillian.

"All right, sweetie," said the cashier.

"She called me sweetie because I was getting all these sweets," said Jillian in the parking lot. Jillian was carrying the plastic shopping bag close to her chest, as if there were no bag. "This is my catch," she said. "Pretty good haul."

Whaaat, thought Megan when Jillian got back to the office with her enormous sack of cookies.

"Hey, girl," said Jillian. "Did you know they have individual Crystal Lights right by the water in the fridge section of Walgreens?"

"What is crystal light?" said Megan. Sounds like a kind of PCP.

"*This* is Crystal Light, you nut," said Jillian, reaching into the sack. She held the marker-sized tube of flavored sugar up to her face and shook it. "It's good."

"What is it, sugar?" asked Megan.

"Yeah, kind of." Jillian sat down and began to spread out her bounty. Megan tried to breathe and just let the universe be and not get involved and not worry about it and just mind her own business and do her job and stuff.

Jillian cracked the Evian, emptied two Crystal Lights into it, and then shook the bottle. It really felt like she was making lunch or something. She set the bottle at a particular distance from her mouse pad and then put the Pop-Tarts and some of the cookies in her file cabinet drawer. This really feels like I've got a stash supply, she thought. She unwrapped the cookie and put as much of it in her mouth as she could and then started laughing.

What the fuck? thought Megan.

Ha ha ha, this cookie is hilarious for some reason, thought Jillian. Mmm, and so good. You know, I heard somewhere that, like, carbs and sugar and stuff can give you a power burst for work. She finished the cookie, washed it down with Crystal Light, and then tested her theory.

"Oh yeah," she said. This works great.

"Oh yeah what?" said Megan.

"Huh?" said Jillian.

"You just said 'Oh yeah.'"

"Oh, you know me, I was just talking out loud."

Now that's how you tempt me, Jillian, if you want to know how to really *tempt* me, if you want to be some kind of a *temptress* for me.

But don't say it.

Jillian started typing rapidly.

Don't say that she means to say "thinking out loud," that the expression is "thinking out loud" and that that's what talking is, communicating or thinking out loud. Talking is always out loud.

Then Jillian started making reminder calls.

Unless it's like money talks or body language.

"Oh, hi! This is Jillian calling from Dr. Schraeder's office! Yeah! Ha ha ha ha, yuh-huh, sure is! I'm just calling to remind you you have a, um, a colonoscopy appointment for next week. Oh yeah, well, we look forward to seeing you then. Ha ha, okay, you too!"

Jillian was using the baby voice and continued laughing after she hung up the phone.

Today is great. Jillian was still floating along. Talking to people is a lot of fun. "Megan, we are so lucky, did you know that?"

"What, you mean to be Americans or something?"

"No, silly. Our jobs. I love my job so much. I just love it

here so much. We are so lucky. We could be working at, you know, a steel mill or something. Sorting grommets. But we have it so nice here. Everyone is so nice here."

Megan turned around and said, "I don't think I would ever work at a steel mill, Jillian."

Jillian reached into her file cabinet and brought out a packet of Pop-Tarts.

"Oh, yeah, but you know what I mean." Jillian's eyes widened, "Mmmm," she sighed. "Oh man, these are so good."

"Pop-Tarts?"

"You want one? They come in packs of two," said Jillian.

"Yeah, I know. But I'm fine with the salad I brought."

God, what? Megan turned around and looked at the colon of a healthy fifty-year-old woman. It was pink and winding. Jillian sighed in the background and Megan tried to force herself to get back on track. I have to file these colons, she thought. That's what I'm doing here. This is important medical stuff.

She filed the woman's colon and switched to the next, which was filled with sludge. Jillian looked at these same pictures all day. This guy was a forty-year-old drinker, smoker, and snacker. It chagrined her to imagine this as the future state of both her and Jillian's bowels. Annoyed her to know that they shared that fate together, probably.

The ninety milligrams of Tylenol T3 with codeine wore off before the day was over. Jillian left the bottle at home because the bottle said not to operate heavy machinery while taking

them and, duh, she knew the bottle meant, like, cars and trac-
tors and stuff, but she would be using a computer all day and
computers were heavy and she was covering her bases. When
she got home she decided it was okay to take one, just one,
because she was in a lot of pain from her accident. The bottle
said TAKE FOR PAIN WHEN NEEDED.

She felt so sad leaving Crispy locked in the bathroom all
day, but that was the only place she could leave the dog where
the poop and pee would be easy to clean up. There it was, it
was gross but it was true and there it was.

"Hey, Crispy!" she said.

She still hadn't gotten Crispy that pull-toy yet and the bath
mat was pretty much shredded.

"Get on out of here," said Jillian, and Crispy obeyed and
started tearing ass around the apartment in circles. Jillian
took a big wad of toilet paper and used it to pick up the turds
and mop up the urine and vomit (which she noticed had some
threads from the bath mat in it, *Crispy!*). She put these wads
in the toilet and flushed and then performed one more wipe-
down of the floor. She fed Crispy and filled her water bowl.

"Do you need to go out?" she asked. Crispy cocked her
head. "No?" Crispy got in the play position. "Okay, I guess
you don't want to go out," said Jillian.

Jillian went to take that one Tylenol, then sat down and
turned on the TV. She was pooped. Elena came over with
Adam.

"Oh, hey, I just got back from taking Crispy on a walk!
Good timing," said Jillian.

"I have to run," said Elena. "Are you coming to the eight-ies party this weekend?"

Jillian looked off into the distance. "Yeah, I guess so," she said.

"Okay, could you come a little early? We need help set-ting up."

"Well, sure," said Jillian. "Yeah, I could do that."

"Okay, I can't pick you up, but you can bring Adam. There'll be an area set up for him and the other kids. We'll have a movie for them to watch or something."

"Oh, yeah, I could bring *Charlotte's Web*."

"That won't be necessary, we have plenty of *VeggieTales*."

"Oh, of course."

"See you Saturday around one o'clock, then?"

"Yeah, and tomorrow, too, right?"

"Yeah. When are you getting your car out of the impound, anyway?"

"Oh, I'm still waiting to hear how much it'll cost, and then I have to set up my court date and everything, but it'll be soon, I promise." This was making Jillian nervous and when Jillian got nervous she got angry and her anger expressed itself in her tone. "So, yeah, I'll definitely be able to come and set up and do whatever you want me to, anytime, you know, okay?"

Elena looked at her and left.

"Gee-whiz," said Jillian. "Gee-whiz, right, Adam?"

"Yeah, gee-whiz," said Adam.

"Who do you like more, Mommy or Miss Elena?"

Adam rolled his eyes.

"Come here," said Jillian. She scooped him up. "Who do you like more, Mommy or Miss Elena?"

"Mommy," he said. He gave her a kiss, then squirmed out of her lap and said, "Crispy!"

Megan could sit now, all her scab did was itch. She sat on the couch and said, "Jillian was totally high all day."

"How could you tell?" asked Randy.

"She was eating cookies and laughing with her mouth full and talking to herself."

"Ha ha ha."

"Being around her makes me feel closer to death."

"Ha."

"It's like, oh-kay, this is the future. Guess I better get used to the idea of slowly going crazy and having a baby and going to some kind of freaky church in the suburbs."

"Oh, come on."

"Easy for you to say, 'oh, come on.' You have a real job and friends and shit."

"Uuuughh," said Randy.

"What? I'm in a dead-end job, this is what it means to be in a dead-end job. I face death."

"You can always get another job."

"Not when I am become death."

"Think positive," said Randy.

In bed that night, Randy put his arms around Megan and said, "Hey, I love you."

"What? I love you, too."

"No, I mean, I really, really love you. You make me happy."

"I know," said Megan. She felt nervous.

"Okay. I just want you to know that I love you and I'm not trying to make you feel bad, but I also, you know, want to have a nice job and active friends and I want to have a girlfriend who is happy at least seventy percent of the time." He hugged her.

"I'm sorry. I get like this sometimes. I'll be better. And you're the only person I really like at all," she said. "So of course I love you." She laughed and it was terrible. "I just feel messed up and diseased right now. But it's just a mental thing, I'll be better, I promise."

"I love you, okay?"

"I know, I love you, too. I'm sorry."

God I suck, god I suck so much I suck so much, what the fuck, why the fuck do I suck this much? Why me? Ha ha ha, why meeeee? thought Megan, feeling the simultaneous sting of remorse and indignation. Oh shit, I'm such an asshole either way.

The next morning when the alarm went off, Megan turned around and squeezed Randy and said "I love you."

"Oh, good morning," said Randy.

She got up and made the coffee and took a shower while Randy stayed in bed and flicked his boner like a doorstopper. She made him a bagel and poured him some coffee and then said, "I made you a freezer bagel. Do you want it in bed?"

They ate together and she left for work, looking pretty damn cute. Usually she looked like she was going to go do some work in total isolation, he couldn't think of where, but she didn't always shower or wear clean-looking clothes. He wondered how the doctors hadn't said anything about it, but then remembered that most doctors' assistants wore pajamas.

He felt a little good about last night, but also a little depressed. He moved to his office with his coffee and looked at the internet for a while. He lit a cigarette and opened the project file for Kelly's store.

He felt a little depressed because she'd said, "You're the only person I really like." He repeated this to himself, and with each repeat he got more and more pissed off. Yeah, pissed off. But then sad for being pissed off. Here is what he thought. If someone truly dislikes "everyone" but one person, that means the person they do like they don't even notice. That person, Randy in this case, is just a blank with no subjective feelings, no interior monologue, no hidden opinion or thought. And that sucked, it was stupid. He was, essentially, her cat.

Her cat who she had sex with and cooked dinner for and watched movies with.

She would have to be nicer.

As soon as he got mad and felt confident about being mad, he imagined what it would be like to say to her that she needed to be nicer. In that conversation there would have to be an "or else." Or else I will have to break up with you. It was depressing to imagine breaking up with Megan, but she was such a fucking drag. He couldn't believe this sloppy, ornery person was his girlfriend.

He stamped out his cigarette and stared at the project file. He had that feeling in his stomach he got when he knew he had to break up with someone. That hollow vacuum feeling. There were always two or three good opportunities to break up with someone in the course of a relationship, and he almost never acted on the first impulse, but once it was there it was never fully gone. He didn't like the way it made him feel. The saying "second chance" came to his mind and he didn't like how condescending it sounded. But it was, ugh, a second chance, in a way, because he understood that people had their phases. But to stay with someone who insulted his existence—acted like he didn't have a full selfhood—was not possible. Impossible.

So she would have to snap out of it.

He thought about getting her a job. She could do pretty much anything, he thought. What he did wasn't that hard, she could do that.

He imagined asking a friend to do her a favor. Then he imagined the friend remembering Megan giving them the stink-eye or something, then he imagined Megan becoming humiliated and infuriated. He dismissed the idea.

She would get out of this phase on her own, he knew it, but he didn't know what role he'd play in all of it. He might not be what was best for her. If she really did hate all of his friends, he couldn't imagine her ever being happy with him.

He got that vacuum feeling again, lit another cigarette, and told himself that it was okay to sit on it for a few weeks, then think it over again. Kelly's website was his priority right now.

4

Adam noticed his mom laughing a lot and thought it was cool. She said she was going to get some cake after work for him to eat for being such a good boy. Elena came over and picked him up. She held his hand as they walked down the stairs and around the block to her car. She held his hand tightly and he kept his hand slack. It was sticky from syrup. He tried to do a dance walk on the sidewalk, but Elena said, "Come on," so he stopped. He added a few spasmodic kicks before they got to the car, but no more full dance walk. Elena liked to listen to the same radio station as his mother did, and she liked to hum along to the songs, too. But her car was totally empty except for a map and a pot of medicated lip balm. Elena pulled into a parking spot, got out of the car, walked around to Adam's door, and then led him into the day-care center.

"Hey, Barb," said Elena. She let go of his hand and he ran off. Elena raised her eyebrows.

"Still no car?" asked Barb.

Elena smiled a sour smile and shook her head. "No, not yet."

Both women shrugged. Adam took up his occupation of the playhouse in the corner. No one was in there yet. He got there earlier than a lot of the children. He crouched in the middle of the house and made a wild face. He held his hands out in front of his face and said "The jaws of life" and then he hissed. He bounced up and down on his legs saying "I am the jaws and the life." He gasped, looked quickly to the side, then prostrated himself on the tight blue carpeting. His hands, the jaws of life, went out in front of him and reached for the plastic walls of the house. He imagined himself as a snake and slinked up to the window and observed all that he could see.

"I don't know, but eventually I'm going to have to ask her to broaden her carpool, you know what I mean? My kids are in high school, I already went through the day-care thing. I'm not trying to do it again with somebody else's baby," said Elena.

"I hear you," said Barb.

"She got brought home by the cops. I'm not trying to raise the child of someone who's in trouble with the law in that way," said Elena.

"Oh, I know. She called in here the other week and practically chewed my head off."

"Why?"

"Why do you think?"

"I don't know."

"The tuition is too high. And I said, 'Listen, lady, maybe that's something you should've thought about before you took a job that didn't pay you enough for all that you need,'" said Barb.

"Oh, my word. I know I'm not trying to be a free car service."

"You know it takes about a thousand dollars to get your car out of the impound."

"It does not!"

"It does too. So, it looks like you got yourself into some charity work."

Elena rolled her eyes. "Even a Christian woman has her limits."

Barb laughed and put her hand on Elena's arm. Adam observed this from his house. The fluorescent lights made the inside of the yellow plastic house glow. More children arrived. Elena nodded while she was talking and kept talking while she walked to the door. Barb laughed and waved, then crossed her arms.

Later, when most of the children had arrived, Adam became involved in a game of house. Julie and Tessa were the mom and the dad and Emma was the baby. Adam was the dog. He sat by the box of toys and watched them make dinner. He chewed on his paws and tried to chew on his haunches but couldn't reach. Mommy and Daddy served Baby some dinner and they all ate the invisible food with their hands. Adam crawled over to them and said, "I love you," and then pawed at the air. The girls giggled and said, "Bad doggie, go eat out of your bowl."

"But I love you!" he said.

"Doggie!" said the dad, and the girls giggled.

Adam looked at Emma the baby. "I'm your sister and I love you!" he pleaded. "Rrruff, I'm your sister, I'm your sister!"

"What are you doing, Adam? Bad doggie, go eat your food," said Tessa.

Adam pawed at the table and at Emma and said, again, but now in a dog voice, "Ri'm rour ristrer rand roi ruff roo!"

He began to pant frantically and flail on the floor.

"Doggie, no!" said the girls.

"I'm a good doggie," he cried. "Woof!"

"Miss Barbara!" said Julie. Adam's eyes widened.

"Woof," he said. He returned to his dog bowl and growled.

Miss Barbara approached the scene. "Yes, Julie?"

"Miss Barbara, Adam is supposed to be the dog and eat his food from the bowl, but he keeps saying he's Emma's sister, but he's still acting like a dog and he's a boy anyway so even if he could be her sister he should be her brother," said Julie.

"Ruh-roh," whispered Adam.

"Adam," said Miss Barbara. "Adam, come."

Adam crawled to her and panted. He sat up on his haunches and put his paws out in front of his chest and cocked his head to the side. "Roi ruff roo," he said.

"Eew!" said the girls.

"Adam, stand up," said Miss Barbara.

Adam panted.

"Adam, stand up."

He stood up.

"Come with me."

The girls giggled.

As Miss Barbara walked him to the other side of the day-care center, she said, "Now, I don't know what it's like being an only child, but a dog is not the same thing as a sibling. Do you understand? You can't play the doggie and say you're someone's sister, it makes you look disturbed. Do you understand? You might not ever understand if you never have a sibling, but that is a sacred bond and a bond that cannot be shared with an animal. It's perverse."

She sat him down at a table and put a coloring book in front of him. "Now I want you to color these pictures in and do a good job."

When she left, he started to mumble "Roi ruff roo" under his breath. "Roi ruff roo."

The image Adam was asked to color was an Easter bunny. The bunny was holding a basket out to him. The basket had eggs in it. The bunny had no background, but he was wearing a waistcoat. Adam picked up a crayon at random and started rubbing it against the paper. It was soothing.

"Roi ruff roo," he whispered, not to the bunny, and not to his family. His family. He looked up at them across the daycare center. He had been abandoned by his family for asking for a higher position. Now they were eating their imaginary food and explaining the events of their imaginary days. Adam continued coloring while he looked at them.

Eventually, they noticed. His sister, Emma, widened her eyes at him and thrust her head forward a few times. A challenge to fight. He sighed and put his cheek in his hand. Sigh. He looked back down at his coloring job of the Easter bunny. "I don't love you bunny, no offense," he said.

Barb was walking around the room with her arms crossed,

surveying all that was hers. All of these children learning about life and social systems and appropriate behavior. Pretty much learning about how things are, and learning it under her gentle guidance. A small boy, Louie, ran past her and she said, "Slow down, Louie." She smiled. So simple. It was all so simple. Separate the ones who are fighting, give light reprimands, subtle suggestions, firm suggestions. So simple.

Meanwhile, Jillian kept getting calls on her cell phone from the same number. She didn't recognize the number and it made her nervous. She reached for a Pop-Tart and waited for Megan to go to the bathroom, then she checked her voicemail. It was the government, wanting to know when she'd schedule her court date, pay her fine, and bail her car out of the impound.

Megan looked at herself in the bathroom mirror. She was a dick. Looking at herself there in the mirror, she knew she was a dick. Only a real dick would have such a lopsided face.

She had to pee soon or Jillian would think she was taking a dump.

After peeing, she looked at herself more. What an asshole, but what to do?

Jillian deleted the voicemails and took another two Tylenol T3s with codeine and decided that the courthouse must have had the wrong number, because she really didn't have the money and wouldn't have the money for another two weeks, at which time she would call the courthouse herself because she was a responsible person.

More dinner? She could make Randy another dinner? A very delicious dinner? She got the impression that something was on the horizon.

At five o'clock, Elena came to pick up Adam and stopped to talk to Barb a second. They talked about how weird Adam was while Adam crawled around on the ground, apparently pretending to be a dog. Barb told Elena about the sister dog thing.

"Ugh," said Elena, throwing her hands up.

"Adam!" shouted Barb. He trotted up to the women.

"Time to go home, sweetie," said Elena.

It was around five, so Megan would be home any second. What a nasty, burdensome feeling. Can you believe it, his hands were sweaty, even though he'd given himself an extension for thinking about this whole thing. "This whole thing." He felt gross.

The downstairs door slammed and he saved his project. Megan walked in with groceries. "Hey, cutie," she said.

Elena thought about how Jillian would probably fuck something up this weekend at the church eighties party. She thought about it in detail, watching Adam fidget in her peripheral vision. She pulled into a parking spot on the street outside of Jillian's apartment building, pumping herself up for the possibility that Jillian would not be home yet. She and Adam would wait inside or maybe she and Adam would take the dog for a walk and she would leave Jillian a note. "You were not here when I got here, and your dog needed out so we took her out." She would not call the dog by its name in the note, she decided. She walked up to the building with the weird, kicking, spasmodic child's limp, damp hand in hers and she wanted to bear down on his pudgy little baby fingers to teach them how to firm up like a normal person's hands.

But Jillian was in, sitting on the couch with that dog. Adam let go of her hand and took a few steps to the side. The house smelled like piss.

"Hey, I just got back from walking the dog, great timing," Jillian said.

Yeah, right.

"You might crack a window in here, the weather's fine," said Elena.

"Oh, I know. I just felt a little chilly on the walk home."

"It's not chilly," said Elena.

"Hmm," said Jillian.

"So, any word on when you're getting your car back? We could really use your help driving this weekend. We need a runner."

"Well, I spoke with the court today and they said my court date is in two weeks, then I should be able to straighten all of this up and get my car back."

"Oh, so you won't have it for this weekend?"

"Nope, it's going to be another two weeks. Hey, Elena, thank you so much for helping me with Adam. You really don't know how much of a blessing you've been to me."

Elena humphed. "It's the least I can do to help."

"It's really a prayer answered."

"Well, just try to get your car back as soon as possible, that'll be thanks enough for me."

"Will do, Miss Elena."

Randy smiled about the groceries, and tried not to let on that he'd been thinking about breaking up with her all day.

Jillian made a shopping list of all the things she needed and then made herself a budget. She needed more toys and, eventually, a dog walker for Crispy and also a crate so she wouldn't have to keep shutting her in the bathroom, and also a proper bed for her. The total for this was about four hundred dollars, which was twice as much as she owed for the fine. Would she have to pay to go to court? Not if she didn't need a lawyer. So no lawyer. And getting the car out, she'd heard, would be about a hundred dollars. But Crispy was a priority. She rearranged her list in order of priorities, toys and the crate came first, then the car business, and then a dog walker.

Maybe she'd be able to get her car back in a month? Ugh. Maybe she could get an extension.

5

The weekend came and Randy thought, We should stay in, but wasn't entirely comfortable alone with Megan since his understanding that things were not going well between them, so he invited their friend David over. This will make her comfortable, he thought. Just two people, where she lives, a low-pressure drinking thing.

David came over and Megan drank two beers quickly.

"How've you guys been?" David asked.

"Eh, fine, I guess," said Megan.

"Pretty good," said Randy. He explained his project for Kelly's store and said he was getting paid for it, and he and David talked about formats for a while, while Megan smoked cigarettes. She tried to interject, but her comments were flaccid. When she spoke, David glanced at her and raised his eyebrows and nodded and then turned back to Randy.

"Where are you working now?" asked Randy.

"Oh, I'm working for Albert."

"Cool, man, I know Albert."

"Yeah, I took a class with him and we really hit it off. It was one of those weird experiences when you have a class and you and the prof both kind of look at each other one day and realize 'We're probably going to be friends.'"

"Ha ha," said Randy. Randy picked up his beer.

"Yeah, that happened to me all the time," said Megan.

"Really?" said David.

Megan shook her head and said she was just kidding.

"Well, Albert sent me an email a few weeks ago and said 'Man, I really liked your writing in class, and I'm looking for a new staff member.' Apparently one of his staffers just got into school in California, so he offered me his job. It's full time. I don't have benefits yet, but he said he's going to work on it."

"That's so cool," said Randy.

"What does Albert do?" said Megan.

"He runs an online design magazine. It's one of the only local design magazines that really matters on a national level." He turned to Randy and said, "You know how stuff is around here."

"So, are you writing about design or are you . . . designing for this design magazine?" asked Megan.

"Oh, Albert likes to do most of the design himself, so I'm writing."

"Oh, right, you said he said he liked your writing from class."

"Yeah," said David. "Actually, the only person he lets help him out with the design is Carrie."

The night plummeted on. Randy and David talked about books they'd been reading and design techniques they liked. They laughed together about mutual acquaintances. Megan drank and smoked and thought about Carrie a little. She thought, I read books and do things, too. But not the same things, and not the same books. Occasionally she interjected, but the things she said were answered with polite questions and did not fit well into the flow of the conversation, so she mostly sat back and tried to relax. She must have spaced out. When she came to, David was saying, "Toothpaste, hacksaw, *People* magazine, a bag of carrots, red gym socks, Jean-Luc Picard, tomato paste, cardboard cutout of Austin Powers, CD player, toothpicks."

"Whoa, cool," said Randy.

"What are you doing again?" asked Megan.

"A memory palace," said Randy.

"It's a medieval memory technique. If you need to remember a list of things, what you do is pick a place that you remember well, like your childhood home or your office or your apartment, and you make a narrative. Like, I walk up my front steps and I step on a tube of toothpaste and I get toothpaste all over my foot, so I pick up a hacksaw and I cut off my foot. Then I open my mailbox and see a copy of *People* magazine that has a photo of me cutting off my foot on the cover. My landlord is standing in my entryway and he offers me a carrot, and I notice he's wearing red gym socks," said David. He kept talking through his memory palace, but Megan was somewhere else.

"Can I try one?" asked Randy.

"Yeah, absolutely." David took a piece of paper and started writing a list.

"This is awesome," said Randy.

Memory palace. Megan opened another beer. She said, "This is awesome," in her head to mock Randy. Then she whispered, "Memory palace."

"You want to try one?" Randy asked.

"Oh, no, I don't think so," said Megan.

They weren't disappointed about it, or outwardly happy. Megan stared at them while they were sitting in silence, Randy looking at the list and David looking at Randy. What's in my memory palace? she wondered. A driveway. One with a basketball hoop on a pole. Megan was eleven and playing with her new friends. They grinned at each other and approached her, tied her to the basketball pole with two jump ropes, attached Rollerblades to her feet, and then drew penises on her face. Her hair was dressed, then, with shaving cream.

Randy recited his list in the background.

They dragged her, on the end of the jump ropes, to a soft-serve ice cream stand and forced her to order them all an extra-large Twister with gummy bears. The guy at the counter was cute—though, in retrospect, he probably was not—and he pointed out to her that she had a penis and the words "I am gay" drawn on her face. As she had not yet learned to be self-deprecating, she had not handled herself well, and she realized, just then on the couch, that she still held a burdensome grudge against those girls for what they had done to her.

She set down her beer and knew she was drunk.

"No, it's cool, guys, I just did one in my head a second ago. A memory palace, I mean," she said. This statement was unprovoked.

"Uh, okay," said David. "Wanna do it for us?"

"Not really."

"Aw, come on, why not?" said Randy.

"You don't want to know what's in my memory palace." But since she was drunk and feeling moved by the rediscovery of the memory, she told them what she had just been thinking.

"That's not really what a memory palace is," said David. "That's just a memory."

"Well, it's the setting of my memory palace," said Megan.

"Yeah, but what were your items?" he asked. Megan looked at him. "And what's the big deal, anyway? Everyone has bad middle-school memories. That just sounds like a little bit of hazing."

"Yeah, well, that's what you say," said Megan.

Randy was annoyed with Megan for moodily describing past social disappointments. And he was well lubricated. "That's not even the worst of Megan's memories," he said.

David laughed encouragingly.

"Honey, I'm surprised you didn't choose your fourth grade living room as the setting for your memory palace," said Randy.

"What happened?" said David.

"I'm sure I don't know what you're talking about," said Megan.

"You know, honey, the time your parents caught you masturbating to cartoons with that—what's it called?—that Dizzy Doodler."

David spit out his laugh. "What is a Dizzy Doodler?" he asked.

"It's one of those," Randy continued, "vibrating pens for children. They draw curlicues, and they're powered by a little motor. Megan used to masturbate with her Dizzy Doodler every Saturday morning while she watched cartoons. Even after she lost the protective cap for the motor in the couch cushions, she kept going. She just had to be more careful when she used it, isn't that what you told me? Didn't you say that one morning you caught an arm of the motor in your underpants and were worried you would someday really injure yourself?"

David was cracking up, and Randy was looking at Megan spitefully.

"He's kidding," said Megan to David.

David waved his hand at Megan and said, "Sure, sure."

"I didn't do that," said Megan.

"One day she got busted and she gave her parents a long-winded speech about how she was addicted to the Dizzy Doodler," said Randy.

"Okay, that's enough," said Megan. "It's not true."

"And how she wanted them to 'THROW IT AWAY!'" Randy mimicked a child's voice. "'JUST THROW IT AWAY! And don't tell me which trash can you use!'"

David was in stitches.

"All right, ha ha, very funny, Randy, very funny," said Megan.

David wiped the tears from his eyes and reached for another beer. "I had a dog once," he said, "who used to lick his penis for hours on end. We were all sure he was masturbating."

"Lovely," said Megan.

In bed, Megan said, "I can't believe you told David about the Dizzy Doodler."

"Oh, he didn't believe me."

"That doesn't matter."

"Come on, I was just teasing."

"That's not the point."

6

Saturday morning came fast. Friday was never a night for events, because Jillian was always so beat. She woke up early and knew that if everything went well today, if she did a good job, things would keep going the way they were going. You know, with Elena helping out and everything.

Jillian made herself a Starbucks by putting coffee, ice, milk, and chocolate syrup in the blender. As the lukewarm, diluted coffee filled her mouth, she thought, How do they do it? She stood there for a full minute in the kitchen, in a trance, with the slippery cup in her hand, before she remembered she was in a hurry. That was the reason she'd made the Starbucks in the first place. Economy of time.

When Adam was dressed and she was dressed, Jillian said, "You wait here, Adam." She took Crispy outside for a second. The dog would not pee, just would not pee at first. Jillian looked at her cell phone to show her frustration, but the dog just would not pee.

"Pee!" said Jillian.

She squatted and whispered "Pee!" again, but Crispy only looked at her and tugged on the leash.

"Ugh, fine, you stupid dog," said Jillian.

They walked around the block.

"You dummy dog," said Jillian.

Crispy wagged her tail and eventually peed and pooped. When this happened Jillian said, "What a good girl, come on! Come on!" and then tried to get Crispy to walk even faster back to the apartment. The poop-bag thing still wasn't happening. Crispy tugged Jillian away from the apartment and got in the play position.

"Silly doggie," said Jillian. Jillian was no fool. Jillian read Crispy's body language, and furthermore knew she wouldn't want to be in the bathroom all day if she were in Crispy's shoes.

"Okay, Crispy," she said when she was getting Adam ready to scoot out the door. "Can you be a good girly?" Crispy stood in the middle of the living room. "She went pee and poop," Jillian said to Adam. "I think we're going to try leaving her out today." Jillian turned on the TV and said, "Be a good girl, okay?" Crispy cocked her head.

It was a twenty-minute walk to the church, which wasn't so bad. Sometimes walking with Adam since they'd decided to stop using the stroller could be tricky, but it wasn't so bad, and they could probably make it on time. She didn't feel like there was any use in taking the bus, and the rates of cabs in the suburbs were outrageous and way out of her budget. They

walked and they saw people working in their yards and playing on the sidewalk, driving their cars and getting in and out
of their cars. Jillian breathed deep of this beautiful morning
air, then accidentally burped a little.

"I love where we live," she said.

Adam was silent, but she interpreted his enthusiastic
dance-walking as agreement.

The church was on a main drag, but there was a nice big
lawn in the back, and the street wasn't all that busy, even
though it was large. Jillian and Adam made their way through
the parking lot, through the front doors, and down the stairs
to the basement, where the party was to be held.

Elena was standing to the side of the room, staring at a
card table. Her arms were crossed and she had one hand on
her chin.

"Hi, Elena," said Jillian.

"Hi, Jillian. Why don't you drop him off in the kids' room
and then come back down here."

"Okay."

They crossed the basement rec room and went up the
back stairs, through a hallway, and into a room that looked
out over the back lawn.

"Oh, you're here early," said Susie.

"Elena told me to get here early. I hope it's okay that I
drop him off."

"Oh, sure. I'm just getting everything all set up for this
afternoon. Hey, Adam, you want to watch some TV and have
some crackers?"

"Yeah," said Adam.

"Okay, we'll be fine up here," said Susie.

"Great!" said Jillian.

She walked back to Elena, who was still looking at the card table.

"What are you looking at?" asked Jillian, as the card table was empty.

"I'm thinking."

"Oh."

"If I gave you a list of things to get, do you think you could get them?"

"Yeah, absolutely."

"Okay." Elena walked to the other side of the basement and bent over another table and wrote a list. Jillian stood where she was, thinking she would do a good job. Elena came over with the list and Jillian looked at it.

"There'll be another list this afternoon, this is just preliminary stuff."

The list included snacks for the party, decorations, and costumes.

"Um, Elena?" said Jillian. "I can totally get this for you, and I'm not trying to be funny, but I don't have a car."

Elena looked at her.

"I just don't know if I can walk to all of these places and carry all of this stuff and get it all done in time for the party."

"Well, I can't come with you."

"Yeah, I know, but, could I borrow your car, maybe?"

Elena stared at her. "Do you have your license?"

"Oh, yeah," said Jillian. Elena gave her a look and Jillian shifted. "Yes, ma'am."

"Okay, you can borrow my car, but if you get pulled over, I don't know if I can be responsible for it."

"Oh, I'm a good driver, don't worry." Elena went to her purse and got out her keys.

"You'll be back before one o'clock, right?"

"Yes, ma'am. I'm just going to go to the drinking fountain to take a Tylenol and then I'm off."

The best route to take was to go to the grocery store, then the party store, then the thrift store for the costumes, but if she did that, then the dips would sit in the car and get warm. She'd have to go to the party store first and get the groceries on the way back. Elena's list had specific directions for the party decorations. Jillian pulled into the Party City parking lot. The store was a warehouse, so she thought she should be able to find everything. Elena wanted posters or hanging boards that said something about the eighties. The list said the posters should say "It's the '80s!" or "'80s Party Time!" Jillian wrinkled her nose at the list. The only decorations she could find with the number 80 on them were birthday posters, and they all had graves and grim reapers on them. That would not do, she thought. There were some paper plates that said "Girls Just Want to Have Fun" and "Girls Night" on them, with pictures of girls in aerobics outfits. They looked kind of eighties.

"Oooh," said Jillian.

She could go through and take out the "Girls Night"

plates, because "Girls Just Want to Have Fun" was an eight-ies song.

She walked the aisles looking for things that would do and put these things in her basket. Neon balloons, neon streamers, neon Puffy Paint, two posters that said "Party" in metallic letters, some blank neon poster board, electric-blue crepe tablecloths, two packages of pink plastic forks, party hats with Michael Jackson on them, and party hats with the Teenage Mutant Ninja Turtles on them.

"This'll do fine," she whispered.

"Okay, your total is sixty-five ninety-eight," said the cashier.

Elena hadn't given her a stipend! she realized.

"Umm," she said.

But Elena would pay her back, and she did have the left-overs from her paycheck in her purse.

She skipped to the car and put the party favors in the trunk. Elena had Yankee Candle air fresheners in her trunk, and absolutely no crumbs embedded in the carpet.

"Mmmm, the cinnamon," said Jillian.

The thrift store was fun, she thought. Her mission there was to pick up some eighties party costumes for the people who didn't wear their own. Just so everyone could feel like they fit in, she guessed. This would be a breeze. She picked out a few for-mal dresses and then a few sweatshirts and some winter gloves.

"Your total is thirty-five dollars," said the cashier. Jillian sighed.

"Whoa-kay," she said.

It was already a little after noon, how did the time fly so

fast? She was running out of money, so she had to cut a few corners, but it would be fine. Instead of the precut carrot sticks she got bags of carrots, and instead of the pre-mixed Hawaiian Punch she got packets of Kool-Aid. Other than that, she stuck to the list (buying the store brand dips and cheese, though, of course, because she had a discount card at that particular grocery store).

She loaded up the car, congratulated herself on not getting pulled over (and totally busted and ruined, but no good to dwell on that!) and getting everything before one o'clock, as she'd been asked.

She went into the church basement with an armload of her spoils and saw Elena there with a few of the other women from church. They were moving tables around and pointing at different parts of the room.

"Oh, thank god, where have you been?" asked Elena.

"Just on the errands. It's before one, isn't it?"

"Okay, bring all of the decorations down so we can get started."

"Okay, hey, Elena, I can get you the receipts for this stuff, can you pay me back tonight?"

"Yeah, sure."

"Cool."

It took three trips, since none of the women offered to help, but in the end it didn't take all that long to get everything down into the basement. When she came down with the last bags of snacks, she noticed Elena looking mad at the bags in the middle of the floor.

"What is all this stuff?" she asked.

"It's the decorations and costumes," said Jillian.

"Yeah, but what's this blank paper for? And there's nothing that says 'eighties.'"

"Oh, there weren't any eighties decorations, so I thought we could, um, make some real quick."

"Jillian, the eighties are really popular right now, are you sure you looked?"

"I looked everywhere, I couldn't find anything." Elena held up the Ninja Turtle party hats.

Jillian said, "Because it's from the eighties."

"Is it? Is it, Jillian? Because my boys watched this show, and they didn't watch it in the eighties."

"Oh, yeah, I'm sure it is. But, look, these are all eighties colors," she said, kneeling down by the bag. "And I got these Puffy Pens." She held a Puffy Pen up to Elena.

Elena sighed. "I just didn't want this to look so amateurish, that's all."

"Oh, no, Elena, it's going to look nice, I promise."

"And what's with all of these sweatshirts? What am I supposed to wear?"

"I thought we could cut off the necks," said Jillian. "And we could make fingerless gloves."

Elena didn't respond. "Carol," she said. Carol came over. "See what you can make of all this."

Elena went off.

"I'm going to make some posters," said Jillian. She picked up the poster board and markers and took them to a corner. She laid out a neon-orange sheet and, in bubble letters, wrote "'80s." She got some tape and taped one of the signs that said

"Party" to the bottom of it. Carol spread the tablecloths out and set out the plates and forks. Jillian walked to the table. She had that nice, floating, hilarious feeling that her Tylenol gave her and she lifted her hands a little high and set them on the plates. She stopped there for a second, then she sorted through the plates and removed the "Girls Night"'s.

She went to the kitchen, chopped the carrot sticks, and mixed the Kool-Aid.

"Oh my, what *is* this," she heard Elena say. Her hands started to tremble when she noticed there was no sugar. She looked from side to side. She went into the hall.

"Melissa," she whispered. She waved Melissa over. "Hey, Melissa, is there any sugar?"

"Hmmm. I know someone was at the store."

"That was me. I forgot to get the sugar."

"I think there are some packets under the coffeemaker."

"Great."

Jillian found a box of Splenda under the coffeemaker. No one will see me, she thought. No one will see me. She tried to turn "No one will see me" into a protective mantra, then she took the box over to the punch bowl and started dumping the packets into it.

Rip dump, rip dump, rip dump, frantically rip-dumping until the punch was a little too sweet, then she mixed it and brought it out to the main room and set it next to the plate of homemade (and wasn't that better?) carrot sticks.

"Can we get this dip put into bowls?" said Elena.

"Oh, yeah, are there bowls in the kitchen?" asked Jillian.

"I really don't have time to check."

"Okay. Hey, do you want me to start cutting up those sweatshirts?"

"Yeah, I called Sandy and she said she has some costume things she can bring. We probably won't need those sweat-shirts."

"Oh, okay," said Jillian.

Everyone in the basement was laughing and taping up streamers and blowing up balloons.

"I think I need you to go on a sandwich run," said Elena.

"Okay," said Jillian. "But I need you to give me some money."

Elena stared at her. "Can't I just write you a check?"

"No, because I don't have a checking account, so if you wrote me a check I'd have to pay ten percent to get it cashed. I need cash or a money order."

"Okay, here's thirty for lunch, that should be enough for some Subway."

"Okay, great," said Jillian.

When she got back with the sandwiches, Elena was mad that the dip hadn't been put into bowls. The party was almost starting.

As Jillian filled the bowls with the dip (she could wait a second to eat her sandwich) Susie from the kids' room came up to her.

"Hey, we have a little problem."

"What?"

"Well, Adam is in the ladies' room and he won't come out."

"Oh, are you kidding?" asked Jillian.

"Nope," said Susie.

The party went until 9:00. At 9:00, Jillian said, "I'm going to run now."

"What, you're not staying for takedown?" said Elena.

During the walk home, Adam looked like he was sleep-walking. Maybe he was.

She opened the door. Crispy had strewn the dirty clothes from the hamper all over the floor and was slowly sucking on the crotch of a pair of Jillian's underwear.

Saturday was no breeze for Megan, either. She woke up and immediately felt embarrassed. That nasty, awful, hollow, end-less embarrassment that was becoming her life. Randy was still asleep. She lay there, wishing she could be unconscious again. If she got up and out of bed, what would there be to do? She could shower and weep and see if that freshened her up. Maybe she could weep while making pancakes and then, with her gelatinous face, walk into the bedroom and say, "I made breakfast, honey, do you want some?" She could make coffee in the French press and imagine every step as the sym-bolic destruction of her soul. Grind the beans, boil the water (she could open her mouth for a silent scream when the teapot whistled—possibly that would be satisfying), and then wrap her fist around the plunger and push those fucking grounds down there where they belonged.

She decided this was a good enough idea. As soon as she was under the water, she started bawling. She sat in the bot-tom of the tub, cried, and washed her feet.

When she got out of the shower, Randy was making coffee in the Mr. Coffee. She didn't want to interact with him until she was dressed, so she walked right past him. Her hair was wet. Her skin felt brittle. Maybe she would be able to go to sleep again.

Randy sighed.

7

On Monday, the phone rang. "Good afternoon, doctors' office," said Megan. "Sure, hold on one second." She put the phone down. "It's for you."

"Who is it?" said Jillian.

Megan shrugged and handed her the cordless.

"Good afternoon, this is Jillian."

"Good afternoon, Ms. Bradley, this is Mike Johnson calling from the county clerk's office, how are you today?"

"I'm doing good, and yourself?"

"I'm well. Ms. Bradley, I'm calling you to tell you that your court date is a week from this Tuesday, on the thirty-first, at eleven a.m. Can you confirm that for me?"

"I'm sorry, Mr. Johnson, but I'm at work right now, and I'm unable to make that confirmation," said Jillian.

"Ms. Bradley, I'm aware that you are at work, but we have been leaving messages on your personal line and we have not gotten a response. If you had called us back, we would have been able to work with you to choose a date, but since you did not return our calls, your date has been scheduled for you. If you do not appear in court on your court date, a warrant for your arrest will be issued and your fine will be doubled. If you are unwilling to pay your fine, which I see here is three years standing, we will have no other option but to take you into custody, and you will have to serve time. I am required by my offices to get confirmation from you for this date."

Jillian had been married once. It didn't work out. She was married when she was twenty-two—seems so young now! It lasted a year and then, after the breakup, Jillian found the lord and everything felt glorious. Really, really glorious, like the way you read about. But then there was, you know, she got lonesome. And then there was this coworker, who was really funny. And the way this coworker would look at her and put her arm around Jillian, it just felt so good to be close to people. And so then Jillian started going out with this girl to dance clubs, and it was silly, but it felt so good. To go into the dark, where it was loud. You really didn't have to think of anything to say. Jillian started going out to buy silky tops with cute patterns on them and a little cinch at the waist, and she painted her nails and did up her face. She went with her coworker to get streaks in her hair, sheesh, it made her feel silly thinking about it. And in the club, when it was dark and the music was loud and everyone was having cocktails, you didn't even have to say anything. She loved that. Everything was in the pre-prep, the preparation. Put on the outfit, have a drink, then (once you were all wound up) let yourself go in the club. And then just look at a guy or see if he was looking at you. And if you felt like it, you could give him a kind of look that you knew he'd be able to read.

And at that time she was taking the pill, so it was okay. She was taking the pill, so if she wanted to have someone real close to her in her bed some night, she could. It was great. But then, you know, it was like how sometimes when you're on a diet and you slip up once or twice. Like, have a donut or a milkshake once or twice, but you're still really on the diet. That was how it got after a while with the pill. She'd slip up once or twice, but then she'd take two the next day, or flush the two or three she hadn't taken, and then it was like, when she looked at the pill pack, she was up to date. A little bit of fudging didn't hurt.

And then there was that night she met that guy and he was dancing close and he smelled good like some kind of cologne and she gave him that unmistakable glance and they took a cab back to her place.

"Condom?" he said.

"I don't have anything," she said. She explained she was on the pill.

I don't have anything, I don't have anything, I don't have anything, for some reason that rang through her head while he put his hand (so big) behind her neck and put his mouth (which tickled) up to her ear.

"Do you have anything?" she asked.

"Nuh-uh," he said and she relaxed so much she wanted to cry. If it weren't for being so riled she probably would have cried. Already they had something in common. Don't have anything, don't have anything. That's great. And he was sweet in the morning. He thought it was cool how she didn't hound him about his number or where he worked he said. She shrugged. I think we have something in common she said. And I think we'll see each other again she said.

The next day and a couple more times she took her pills, but then, since she wasn't really going out that much, she stopped taking them.

It was in the parking lot of a Walmart (of all places!) she figured out she was probably pregnant. It was this feeling, it was a creepy feeling, like something from somewhere else was communicating with her. Like a ghost? Kind of like a ghost? Because it was this, like, this thing that was going to happen and that couldn't be stopped (a force?) and it was just, you know, tapping her on the shoulder for a second to say "Hi" and "I'm going to be here soon."

She went into the Walmart and bought a betta fish.

But he was lying when he said he didn't have anything, because he did have something, he had a girlfriend who he lived with, and that seemed like sort of a lot. She asked around to find that out, and she asked around to find out his number, and when she called he said that it was okay because he and his girlfriend had an agreement about things.

This was not true, it became clear after not too long. She had a few months where she thought maybe there would still be some kind of a possibility for her and him to get together, but then it was clear that there wasn't. So then she went back to the church, had her baby, and now here she was.

"Ms. Bradley, do I have confirmation?"

"Yeah," said Jillian and she hung up the phone.

Why do we do it to each other? All of this girl-on-girl *vio-lence*? Well, not really violence in the strict sense, she'd never been in a real fight, but a type of primitive aggression she felt constantly, yes, she really felt it was constant.

It was one of Carrie's days off and she was in her apart-ment, looking at her nail polish and musing. Her roommates were at work. She loved her roommates, she really did, they were dolls, but she even felt it from them. She was the kind of person who liked to feel comfortable with people. She couldn't help it, it was her personality.

It was like, she thought, she just wanted to let all of these women know that there was no shortage of ejaculate on the planet and that they could, you know, share it.

"That's gross," she said and shook her head and stood up from the couch. She walked around the apartment. She walked to Janet's door and nudged it open with her toe. Carrie thought Janet was some kind of a genius. She walked to Janet's closet and poked through her clothes, then walked back to the couch and resumed the examination of her nail polish.

No one ever wanted to share clothes anymore.

She wanted to make a database. When she thought of the database, she became slightly nervous. Not overly nervous, but a little nervous. It was an idea she'd had in the back of her head for almost two weeks now and she wasn't able to pin down what, exactly, the database would be, what it would contain, or from where it would be accessible. But it would be some kind of database. She'd stopped looking at her fingers and was staring in the direction of the bay windows.

About once a month she felt nervous, and when she felt

this way she had to remind herself that what she was doing was important. It's hard to put yourself in historical perspective, but it can be really helpful, too, and you really need to do it. She was a part of a cultural movement and a part of a community that was directly responsible for the way the world would work in the future. She repeated this idea. There, now she felt better.

Maybe the database would have something to do with her ideas on the American workplace. Those were ideas she hadn't been able to use in her artwork yet. She loved those ideas and knew they were important. People were living in traps of their own habits. People should get up and walk around in the office. They should be able to move their desks, switch cubicles with a friend, use the floor as a chair and the chair as a desk, lie down on their stomachs to stuff envelopes, review the quarterly earnings on a park bench, weather permitting. She knew this kind of re-imagining was essential to the vitality of the American people, and she was lucky (but was it luck, or had she worked to get where she was?) to work for Jill, who would definitely let her try any and all of these new techniques.

Carrie sat on the couch, staring at the bay windows with her left hand held out absent-mindedly before her. Soon it would be 3:30, soon it would be 4:00, soon it would be 4:30, soon it would be 5:00, then 5:15, then 5:30, then 5:45, 46, 47, 48, 49.

PART 3

PART 3

1

"There I was in my storage unit. I had nothing, no job, no boyfriend, no place to live, and then, BAM, six weeks later I had my career, and six years later here I am," said the drug rep, who was standing in the waiting room and leaning on the counter. She had a miniature cart with a few crates and boxes on it, the sort of rig a homeless person would have, but new looking, as if she wiped it down every night and got the wheels and buttons repaired from time to time. Megan thought the whole drug-rep thing was disgusting, corporate, and transparently evil, but Jillian stood on the other side of the counter smiling at the rep with her mouth open.

"Wow," said Jillian.

The drug rep looked like she took street-fighting classes.

"Yeah," said the drug rep.

"You know, I was trying to start my own business," said Jillian.

"Oh, really, what's that?"

"I was going to do coding. I found the software and every-thing, but things just didn't quite work out."

"Awwwww," said the drug rep. "You know, honey, I could always hook you up with a job in my business."

"Oh, yeah?" said Jillian.

Megan could not believe this. It was inappropriate to talk about wanting to quit or switch jobs when you were at your workplace and nine feet away from your employer.

"But I should warn you, it's real fast-paced."

"Well, maybe I'll think about it," said Jillian.

I mean, if Megan could resist it, everyone should be able to.

"Okay, sweetheart, I'm going to leave these samples with you, and you just give me a call whenever Dr. Billings is ready to meet with me."

"Oh, okay," said Jillian, taking the samples.

"Can I leave some literature out?" asked the rep.

"Sure," said Jillian.

By "literature" the rep meant advertisements for bowel-emptying medication.

Jillian's smile was like stuck or something. She almost started laughing, but she knew it would be a deep, woofing, slow laugh. Ridiculous. Thinking about laughing like that al-most made her laugh again, a high-pitched rapid giggle. Ultimately she didn't laugh, she just stood there and watched the drug rep wheel her little hobo cart out of the lobby.

Jillian walked back to her desk and said, "That woman is such a sweetheart."

Megan didn't respond, but Jillian was used to that.

Jillian could feel that her mouth was still open. The T3s

were getting less and less effective, not that they were so super effective in the first place. She still felt a lot of pain, you know. But now there was a weird grating feeling inside. Not the inside of her body, because she couldn't locate the grating feeling in any one of her organs. It was like the Tylenol or whatever was starting to grate at her soul.

When this occurred to her, her hands started darting around her desk. She picked up and set down her mouse, ran her fingers over the pens in her pen cup, and typed a few blurts of nonsense on her keyboard, which made the computer *bonk-bonk* with the error sound.

My soul is messed up now, she thought. She was terrified.

She reached for a Pop-Tart, it was the last Pop-Tart. Oh, that's perfect. If that's not perfect! It's like I'm down to my last Pop-Tart! She tried to recall some mantras, but she felt like she always messed them up a little bit and then she became frightened that this feeling inside of her came from reciting a devotional incorrectly and now, because of that, she was in serious, terrible trouble.

She unwrapped the Pop-Tart with shaky hands and tried to let her mind wander.

There was something about the siding for the house of the soul . . . God, what was it? Something about if you smile at someone, their smile will shine back into you? God, what was it?

"I'm going to go get some coffee," said Megan.

"Oh, sure," said Jillian.

After Megan left, the phone rang.

"Good afternoon, doctors' office," said Jillian. "Oh, sure.

Dr. Schraeder sees patients on Tuesday mornings and Thursday afternoons. Her first available appointment is one-thirty on the sixth."

"Well, don't you have anything sooner?" asked the man on the line.

"No, I'm sorry, that's the earliest availability."

"Well, I'm having some pretty severe symptoms over here, and I don't think I can wait a week and a half to come see the doctor," said the man.

"I'm sorry, sir, but if this is a medical emergency, I'd recommend going to the emergency room."

"I'm not going to wait two hours in the emergency room just to have them refer me to my own doctor, okay?"

"Okay, I understand that, sir. I understand that this is frustrating, sir."

"And I work on Tuesdays and Thursdays, so I'm going to need to see the doctor on a Monday or a Saturday," said the man.

"I'm sorry, sir, that's not possible."

"Why is that not possible? Isn't Dr. Schraeder a professional who cares about the well-being of her patients?"

"Yes, sir, I'm sure she cares about your well-being."

"Well, it really doesn't seem that way, the way I'm being treated right now. This is just inconscionable, you know. It's inconscionable."

The man was starting to squawk a little and raise his voice.

Jillian didn't know what inconsciousable meant, but she had a few guesses.

"Sir, okay, maybe if you could tell me some of your symptoms, I could pass them along to Dr. Schraeder, and then maybe she would be able to fit you in sooner."

"Well, are you a nurse?"

"No, sir, I am the office manager."

"Well, if you're not a nurse or if you don't have any medical training, I don't know why I should tell you any personal information about my health life. Isn't that illegal?"

"Sir, I assure you I signed a HIPAA confidentiality form when I was hired, and I take my job very seriously, and I would not betray your privacy, sir."

"How do I know you're not lying? Listen, missy, I want to talk to Dr. Schraeder right now, or I'm going to hang up."

"Sir, please calm down. Dr. Schraeder is not in the office today. I promise you the best way to get in touch with her is to leave a detailed message with me."

"Well, how are you going to relay the message to her? I want you to give me her cell phone number."

"Sir, I'm sorry, but I'm not allowed to give out any of her personal contact information."

"If I hang up, I'm going to call back and get you fired."

Jillian wished he would, and almost said, "Oh, go ahead, whatever, please just do it."

"Sir, could I please have your name and telephone number?"

"I already gave you my name. You should have my telephone number there in my chart."

"Sir, I apologize, but I don't recall your name."

"You say you're the manager? Well, this office is damned,

then. What kind of a secretary doesn't take notes during a phone call?"

"Sir, I am not a secretary, I am an office assistant, and the office manager."

The man hung up.

That was it.

"No, I'm sorry, I don't remember talking to anyone like that. I'm sorry, I'm sure I would have let you know if I spoke with someone who got that upset."

Or, "Sir, no, I'm sorry, I don't think we've spoken before. The office manager? I don't think we even have an office manager."

The mantra was something about keeping up appearances and believing that God would make things right again and that you shouldn't be upset or act like anything is wrong because that might bring someone else down or make them upset. It was about acting like you were already in the place you wanted to be in or something. She couldn't remember the exact line, but the sentiment of it came back to her, flooded her with the approximation of its meaning (vivid, this feeling, clear and strong, but impossible to pin down, you know, just like God was, so that was okay and was a comfort) and then suddenly she knew everything would be okay. She addressed the grating feeling in her soul and told it (her soul) that this feeling would not be around for long, or forever, and that things would be back and up and in working order in a jiff.

She almost vomited.

Megan came back in with a cup of coffee.

"Hey," she said.

"There were no calls while you were out," said Jillian.

"Okay," said Megan.

Later on in the day, near the end of the day, Jillian said, "Oh, hey, Megan, I just wanted you to know that I'm going to be out of the office on the thirty-first, okay?"

"Uh, yeah, that's fine."

"Because I have a court date."

"Okay."

"It's for child support payments. I'm going to see if I can get my ex to start helping me out with day care and stuff. It's eight hundred dollars a month, can you believe that?"

"Uh, no, wow, that's more than twice my rent."

"It's absurd. And with all of the toys and clothes and stuff, and things for the dog, it really adds up, you know?"

"Yeah, I guess so. That's just one of the reasons I'm glad I don't have pets or children."

"Yeah, what are the other reasons?" asked Jillian. There was heat in her voice.

"Time. Also time. And, uh, I guess the idea of being pregnant and having a baby grosses me out."

Megan shifted uncomfortably in her chair.

"Oh, no, it's wonderful! It's hard, but it's so great. You'll be a great mom someday, just you wait."

What does she think she's saying to me? thought Megan. Megan wanted to stand up and hysterectomize herself with the letter opener while screaming and then throw her uterus at the wall above Jillian's desk just to show Jillian how wrong she was about that.

"Yeah, I don't think I ever want children," said Megan.

"Awww," said Jillian.

Do you pity me? thought Megan. *You* pity *me?* She tried to rein herself in.

"Hey, what kind of coffee'd you get?"

"It's just black coffee," said Megan.

"Ugh! Gross! Ha ha, you don't like to get anything sweet in your coffee?"

"No, I think cream and sugar in coffee is gross."

What a stupid, predictable conversation.

But Jillian thought maybe it wasn't such a bad idea, asking her ex for some money.

The next day, Jillian said, "Doctor, can I talk to you for a sec?"

"Uh, sure, said Dr. Billings.

"I'm going to be out of the office next Tuesday, it's un-avoidable."

"Sure, that's fine with me."

"I have a court date," said Jillian.

"Okay," said Dr. Billings.

"It's for child support."

"Okay."

"I'm going to tell Dr. Schraeder, too, I just thought you'd like to know, because sometimes I answer your phone calls when Megan is busy with something else."

"Yeah, Jillian, it's fine."

"Okay, good."

Megan heard this and thought it was a dig. Dr. Schraeder came in an hour later and Jillian gave her the same spiel.

"Yeah, whatever," said Dr. Schraeder. "Whatever you need to do."

Jillian smiled and walked back to her desk.

Ugh, thought Megan.

The doctors started seeing patients.

"I'm going to make reminder calls for tomorrow," said Megan.

"All righty," said Jillian.

Megan started making the calls.

What if I called him right now? thought Jillian. That might not be such a bad idea, you know. She's making calls, I could just call him right now real quick.

She got an electric feeling when she thought to call him, like maybe this time it would go okay. He was the last person she'd had sex with. But she'd had enough sex, that wasn't what the feeling was about.

Oh, man, what a crazy idea. Her heart started going crazy, and she got an adrenaline rush. Everyone in the waiting room was taken care of, and Megan was on the phone. She could stick the call in real quick. She didn't have the energy to call him at night, and also she had to watch out for the dog and the kid at night. There was something neutral and encouraging about the office. She held the phone, her cell phone, out in front of her and almost started laughing that low, barking laugh again, like vomit-laughing, while she looked at her phone and thought about calling.

No matter that she'd deleted his phone number from her contacts three years ago, those numbers were burned in her brain and they would never leave. Sometimes she thought she'd see those numbers on her death bed while she was going over all the stuff that had made up her life, but that was stupid.

Abruptly, she dialed his number and slapped the phone to her cheek.

His voicemail.

"Hey, it's me, Jillian. I just had a couple of quick questions about Adam, like, an update or something, so give me a call when you get this. Okay, thanks."

She hung up, set the ringer to vibrate, and put the phone in her pocket. The way she said the message was okay. It sounded nice and like she wasn't a crazy lady, but it had come out too fast. He'll just think I'm in the middle of something and that I figured he'd have his voicemail on. He'll think I'm busy and that's why I was talking so fast.

She tried to do some work, but she knew he'd call back, since it had been almost a year since she'd called him. She knew that when she called him too much he was unlikely to respond, but she knew, she really knew, that since she hadn't been abusing their connection—you know, Adam—that he would probably call her back.

No, he would definitely call her back, since she hadn't been calling him all the time. It had been a year, and she deserved to be called back.

He called back. Her phone started vibrating while she was thinking. It was a bad sign that he'd called back so quickly.

"Hi," she said.

"Hi," he said.

"I guess I had some questions about Adam."

"Yeah, I got your message."

"Well, so, here's the thing. My car is damaged from a deer accident, and I don't have enough money to get my car fixed *and* pay for Adam's day care this month. And, also, I work in the city, so I've been taking the train to work and a woman from my church has been driving him to day care, and so I really do need my car."

The guy sighed on the other line and said, "I told you a long time ago that I didn't have any money, and if the reason you wanted to have this kid was to get money from me, it wasn't going to work, Jillian. Don't you remember that?"

"Yeah, I remember. I guess I just thought you might be interested in the welfare of your son."

"Well, I just don't have anything."

Jillian began to feel that rage again that she got when she talked to him. Somehow she always forgot about it. That feeling like she just wanted to get her hands on him and sink her fingers into his skin and pop out his eyeballs and mash his genitals and rip off his fingers and shove them up his nose and into his brain to try to get him to be a decent person and act like they had some kind of humane, caring understanding.

"So what am I supposed to do, leave him at home all day? Bring him to work? Or should I just take him out back and shoot him in the face with a shotgun?" she asked.

"I don't understand why you're getting so emotional, Jillian. Nothing has changed. Nothing in our agreement has changed."

"But don't you care at all?"

"This isn't about whether or not I care. I wish you wouldn't make this about that. I wish you wouldn't attack me in this way, it's not fun. I called you back because I thought you were trying to be friends with me, and I was interested in that."

"You know, I am interested in that. I would like for us to get along, but right now I just . . ."

"I really don't think you're ready for friendship. Every time you talk to me, it's some demand. Don't you see why I wouldn't want to be around that? We don't know each other well enough for me to put up with that."

Jillian wanted to start crying or screaming, but unfortunately she couldn't do either.

"I just thought you would like an opportunity to help out your son," said Jillian.

"No, that's not what's going on here. You want me to pay to fix your car."

Megan couldn't hear the other end of the conversation, but she knew Jillian was talking to her ex and therefore she knew (by the nature of their conversation) that Jillian did not in fact have a child-support court date next week.

"Which I believe proves, not that you care," she said later that night to Randy, "that she is a hysterical, pathological liar."

"Okay," said Randy. "But I still don't see why you care so much."

"I care so much, Randy, because the way this woman behaves is completely disgusting."

"Yeah, well, so she lied. So what? She's embarrassed. She doesn't want her employers and coworkers to think she's a criminal. I get that. I understand it."

"Yeah, okay. But I guess what I haven't been able to communicate is, I mean, I get why she wouldn't want to be thought of as a criminal, but I think she does want to get caught. Either that or she's just a total moron. Why would she wait until *after* telling everyone that she had a child-support court date to call her ex and ask him for money? And loudly. There's a lot at stake. She lied to get codeine, too, and she's been taking it at work."

"I don't understand why you care," said Randy.

"It's disturbing, that's why! Because she does these elaborate performances, like chewing her ex out and asking for painkillers, but on the other hand she acts like no one is watching. That's it. Everything with her is an act, but she behaves like her acts are invisible to everyone."

"Ah, if only she knew," said Randy. He cleaned some crap from underneath his toenail.

"She's practically shitting on the floor," said Megan.

"Mmm-hm," said Randy.

"It's like, don't you finish concocting worlds like that when you're fifteen?"

"What worlds?" Randy asked. He was thinking about how much longer he and Megan would stay together.

"The parallel worlds in which the lies aren't lies," said Megan. "It's like, I remember I didn't do some project on dinosaurs or whatever in sixth grade, so a week after it was due, I broke into my science teacher's room and stuck my paper into the stack of graded papers. And then I convinced myself that she must have just overlooked it, and practiced how I would say 'that's strange, I wonder why you didn't grade it?' That's what Jillian is doing, but she's not a child. She *has* a child, and it's terrifying to think of her in charge of something that fragile when she's living in a delusional reality!"

"What happened with the dinosaur paper?"

"It doesn't matter," said Megan. "I don't remember. It doesn't matter." She picked up her beer and drank from it.

2

Jillian went into the bathroom that night and sat on the floor and cried while she listened to the radio. When the commercials came on, she felt self-conscious and had to stop crying for a second, but then when the music came back on she cried again. She did this for twenty minutes. The bathroom smelled like dog urine.

Amanda was at home, thinking about sending Megan an email.

The email would say something like, "I'm sorry we got into a fight, but I don't take back anything I said, because I really do think you have a huge problem that you need to snap out of or you're going to find yourself without any friends someday very soon."

But then she found herself saying things like, "Or has that day already come?" out loud to herself in her bedroom in a gravelly voice, and found herself cocking her head to the side and furrowing her brows while she said more things like, "I mean, who do you think you are?" so she decided maybe she wasn't ready to write Megan an email, and she didn't want to do it if her heart wasn't in it.

She couldn't stop thinking about Megan, it was becoming kind of an obsession. To be fair, a part-time obsession. She didn't lose sleep over it or skip work because of it, but still. When her mind had a free moment to wander, and there were a surprising number of those in the day, it went to Megan, and Amanda replayed the fight they'd had, and she replayed her victory over Megan, and that only fueled her thirst for another victory. She wanted to reform Megan, get her to stop whining and get a better job and be more friendly. Maybe get her out of the house? Maybe her relationship was bad? Maybe they could start jogging together?

Probably not.

And why hadn't Megan written to apologize for being a dick? And blah-de-blah and on and on.

Jillian wiped her face and left the bathroom to make dinner. She made a Healthy Choice microwave dinner for herself, something with chicken, and made a child's microwave dinner for Adam, something with mac and cheese. After dinner, Jillian poured herself two bowls of cereal. She sat in front of the TV and she didn't have any money, and the dog and Adam had no idea that meant they didn't have any money, either. It was weird to look around and see nice carpet, a kid, and a dog, all in the glow of a TV, and to have a full stomach, but to know she had no money. Maybe she would start smoking again. She got up from the chair and got an oatmeal cream pie from the cupboard and ate it in the kitchen, threw away the wrapper, poured herself a glass of D milk, and went back to her chair.

The next morning, Elena drove to Jillian's house listening to Christian rock and feeling happily superior. That was the only reason she did this, and she was old enough to be honest with herself about it. She was a hardened older lady, and she knew she helped Jillian because it gave her pleasure to have Jillian on the end of her hook and at her mercy. It gave her pleasure, also, to witness Jillian's life, which she had heard about in great (if muddled) detail at church healing groups, which she often led. Jillian's life was shitty, and Jillian didn't know how to improve it because she was too stupid.

Elena was old enough not to lie to herself about the way she really felt about things.

Jillian was the kind of person who went for the short fix instead of the long fix. She knew nothing about sacrifice and never would, and it was a pleasure for Elena to watch Jillian fail, because Jillian's way of life stood in opposition to Elena's. It wasn't that Elena didn't want two cookies and a bag of chips with lunch, just to grab an obvious example of something symptomatic, but she knew it would rot her body, so she abstained. Elena delighted to hear Jillian talk about her plans to diet, because she knew that Jillian was too weak and was all talk. That was another thing that Elena wasn't, and that was all talk. If she wanted to volunteer at a homeless center, she did it. She forwent the "Oh, how nice of you"s she knew she'd get if she told her friends as soon as the idea came into her head, and the reward for this tight-lippedness was a solid, sturdy respect that was given to a woman who was so humble and selfless that she didn't even ask for congratulations, but just went out to the homeless center and volunteered.

Elena noticed that she smelled like Woolite. Jillian will smell like baby burp, even though she doesn't have a baby, thought Elena.

Elena drove with nice posture. She parked, she got out of the car, she walked up the stairs, and she made no plans. With an upper hand like Elena's, there was no need to rehearse. Not with someone like Jillian, at least. It was like talking to a filth-covered child.

She had keys, but out of the appearance of politeness, she rapped curtly on the door several times and heard, "Oh, hey, I unlocked it, come on in!" from the other side of the threshold.

"Are you about ready, Jillian?" asked Elena.

"Oh, I'm running a little late, but Adam's ready. I still have to take the dog out."

"Hmm, okay. Adam!" Adam walked to her like he was walking to the gallows. If he were her son, she would tell him to stand up and show some respect or some grace or dignity, but he was Jillian's son, so his behavior was meaningless. He was a way for her to bond with Barb from Sunnyside Up. Their banter had been solidifying into a friendship, and she looked forward to seeing Barb again. So, there you go. That was another reason to like helping Jillian.

"When will your car be out of the impound?" Elena asked.

"Oh, uh, I have a court date next week, so I'll get it out when I have my court date next week."

"Okay, good," said Elena. "What day?"

"My date is on . . . Tuesday."

"All right," said Elena. "I've been planning on going out of town for a while, but I haven't been able to since I've been helping you out." Elena was just riffing. "So I'm going to plan to be out of town on Wednesday, then, that's great news for me, Jillian." Elena ushered Adam to the door, but slowly. She was waiting for it.

"Um, okay," said Jillian. That tension in her voice was so rewarding, that little bit of attitude, that little bit of aggression, but the absolute understanding that there was no way to give it vent and that she, Elena, was essentially impervious.

"I guess if you don't have your car by then, you'll have to find someone else to drop him off," she said. Then she left.

Jillian, for the fourth or fifth time in her life, realized she was capable of murder.

"Can we listen to something else?" asked Adam.

"No," said Elena. "I'm doing you a favor, and you'll listen to my radio."

"I get to listen to my music, usually," said Adam.

"Well, I don't have any of your music," said Elena.

"Can we get some breakfast?" asked Adam.

"Didn't your mother give you breakfast?"

"No, we didn't have time," said Adam.

Elena felt like a kidnapper. She could imagine herself

driving Adam out to the woods and drowning him in a creek or knocking him unconscious and burying him alive (even if he did dig himself out, what would he do then?) and then driving home. Who would people believe? She would tell her husband that Jillian wasn't at home, no one was, wasn't that weird? so she just came home. Then she would say hateful things about Jillian, just to not seem suspicious. And who would they believe? Why would Elena murder the child? Jillian was like a frightened hamster, with every reason to snuff out her own youth. It would be an easy setup.

She pulled up to the day-care center after that thought and remarked to herself that the drive had seemed faster than usual.

Gosh, was it Friday already?

3

Randy got back from Kelly's late that night and was giddy about the website, which they had just "launched" or whatever. Randy showed it to Megan and it looked like any old shit and, god, what was wrong with her, she couldn't even fake it anymore. She couldn't even say some stupid shit like "I'm so proud of you" or even "Good work, baby" with a fucking kiss or something. She gave the web page a tight-lipped, condescending smile (eyebrows raised) and said, "Wow, you got that finished quickly."

"Yeah, I guess," said Randy, who definitely thought she was being bitchy, but he didn't really care that much anymore (because it was too much worry to care, you know, he hadn't even looked to see if she had some kind of massive, sexy scar on her asscheek; that was how much he really just didn't give a shit anymore). "You excited for the party tomorrow night?" he asked.

"Oooh, right," she said. "The inaugural BBQ."

"Are you going to comb your hair for it?"

"We'll see," she said.

Why did she want to stab him in the face so badly and so suddenly, too? He misunderstood her. That was the insult. He thought he understood her, but the way he understood her was so simple and condescending, and that made him an idiot. If she were hearing about this, she would obviously side with herself, and then anyone who acted contrarily would become the object of her scorn, her dismissal, whatever.

She wanted to say "Fuck the police" because yeah, she didn't need anybody. Fuck the police. She looked at him contemptuously. Fuck the police, fuck the motherfucking po-lice, motherfucker.

Jillian was feeling nervous about the coming week. She kept pacing around and eating handfuls of cereal. She did not have any money. She would not be able to get her car. If she got her car, she would not be able to pay for Adam's day care. If she got Adam's day care, she wouldn't be able to get him there. She was going to have to rob a bank or sell her couch or something. Pacing. She kept pacing. That's it, maybe. Adam and Crispy were watching TV. She brought her laptop into the living room to be with them and started looking at craigslist to see what kinds of prices she could get for her stuff. She would take pictures of all of her stuff and put them on the internet and have people come over and pay her for it. She had too much shit, anyway.

She spent a few hours on craigslist and then almost started crying because it seemed like it wasn't going to work. And plus, how was she supposed to live like a normal person without a couch or a table or clothes? Anyway, her stuff was so fucked up and junky, and half the people on this website were giving their stuff away. Free for pickup? What was that shit? She saw more stuff on there that she thought she might like to grab (if she had a car) than stuff that looked like hers selling at an encouraging price.

Her kid and dog were passed out because it was, like, two in the morning. She was agitated. Oh my god, so agitated.

The first thing Megan noticed when she woke up on Saturday was that she was covered in a film of sweat. She had beads of sweat on the bridge of her nose. When she reached up to touch her face, her fingers slipped. The leaves that had been growing on the trees in the background (in the background, I guess, of the events of her life) were suddenly very apparent. The light in her bedroom (which she shared with Randy, who was still asleep and probably too dull in the head to appreciate this strange new change) was green. It was green because it was coming in through the leaves on the trees. She was more than happy to get up and away from Randy, who she now currently hated.

It was like all of a sudden the change had happened. She wasn't even aware of spring. And she was surprised, the way she was surprised last year, that she was surprised that it was

hot again. Oh, right, heat, she thought. She was wearing flannel pajama pants. She thought about taking them off, but she
didn't want to take her pants off in front of Randy. She put
shoes on, poured herself a glass of water, and left the apartment. Fuck you, Randy.

It looked like it was going to storm. There was that light
that comes from electricity in the air. How did she know that?
Probably wasn't even true, she was just pretending to know
the causes of things, bullshitting even in the privacy of her
own mind. What a weird walk, but a great idea, because it
was summer now, and that meant an increase in personal
freedom. She would probably be back before Randy was
awake, and maybe she wouldn't even tell him she'd gone on a
walk. It was, like, eight in the morning. Usually she slept until
ten-thirty on Saturdays, so these couple of hours were extras.
Everything was so green. She drank the water and saw a fully
clothed woman walking on the opposite side of the street.

Jillian woke up drenched in sweat. I'm disoriented, she
thought. She walked out into the apartment, which had
stopped being clean awhile back. There was a look to the air
that was familiar, holy shit it was summer. Jillian went around
and shut all the windows and turned on the AC. She was
drenched. She got into the shower. While in the shower, she
thought she might as well pick up a little bit today. Her body
ached, but she wouldn't feel the full force of her predicament
until after noon, and she would take that as a blessing from
the lord.

It was really, like, eighty-five degrees outside already. Megan wasn't wearing underpants and her asscrack was sweaty. She stopped feeling liberated and started feeling exposed out in the world in her pajamas. Slime under her tits, too. The light outside was so beautiful. When she thought about going back inside to clean up and get dressed, she wanted to die! Oh, yes, to die! She laughed. It was dark in that apartment and dirty and it was small, it was incredibly small, and she wasn't in the mood to be so close to someone like Randy.

She thought about "walking forever" in an abstract way, but she'd tried stuff like that before. About two hours was as much as she could take before getting depressed.

It was a weird feeling, this feeling. It was a dead-end feeling, but the dead-end feeling came from, like, the possibility of eternity. She knew she would give up everything in her life to exist in the first twenty minutes of this walk, but that was impossible, and at some point she would have to go back inside, and then the grips of her crappy mood would start in again. She wanted to do one more thing before she went in, though.

Jillian got dressed in jeans and put all of the dirty dishes in the dishwasher, all the trash in the trash, and all the dirty clothes in the hamper. She woke her kid up and they walked the dog to the Starbucks.

Megan couldn't think of anything to do. She thought about eating a leaf, but that seemed stupid. She decided to lie down in a median for a minute. If she happened to fall asleep, then maybe that would be amazing.

Pretty much, she wanted to be gone so long that Randy would worry about her. She wished she could go away and be completely alone for five years. Or she wished she would die.

"No dogs in Starbucks, ma'am."

"Well, could I use the drive-through?"

What would be the most just vehicle to wrest me from this mortal coil? A Vespa? Yes, I want to be hit in the neck with the front tire of a Vespa, that way my face won't be covered by a car when I die. I'll be able to see this beautiful sky and this weird green light, which I have decided I want to be the last things I see.

By the time Jillian, Adam, and Crispy were almost back home, Jillian felt nasty. Her entire shower was undone. It was really, really hot out.

Eventually, Megan got up. When she sat up in the median, the head rush felt similar to crying. She was depressed. She said "I'm depressed" and sat there for a minute longer, but then she had to stand up and walk back home. It was weird walking home, because she partly wanted to go home, but why? What is there for me? I hate it there so much I want to murder someone.

She held out her hands and looked at the mulch imprints on her palms.

These hands. These hands! I am capable of it, with these hands. She made gripping claw shapes with her hands. "I fucking hate myself and my liiiiiife," she said, there on the sidewalk in her flannel jammy pants, looking at her hands, sweating, walking, and talking to herself like a fucking ass-hole. She had abandoned her water cup.

I would so much rather cry. I would so much prefer this if I could just start bawling and screaming here in the street. Maybe I could pretend to be so fucking crazy that someone would call someone else and then that second person would come with an ambulance and I could act so crazy that they'd have to take me somewhere with a green lawn and give me a shower and put me in a straitjacket (which actually sometimes seems like it might be comforting, if a person had a little bit of choice in the matter) and I don't have a wallet or even un-derpants on, so no one would be able to tell me to go home, and then eventually someone would see me on the news and be like "Isn't that Megan?" and then Randy would feel like an asshole and I would get to go live with my parents for a while and it would be a judgment-free zone because everyone would be a little bit afraid of me, but they would finally see that I was a person worthy of their sympathy. If I threw myself down on the street and started screaming like a freak in my jammies then people would see, and then it would be all right, you know? You know? You know?

"You know?" she whispered. "You know?" She whispered it while she looked at the palms of her hands and walked back to her apartment in the apocalyptic green light, wondering what she could do to convince people that she was crazy (therefore a victim) and not an asshole (therefore just an asshole).

"Where *were* you?" asked Randy.

"It's so fucking dark in this shithole," said Megan.

"Where were you?"

"What a dump. Hey what's that from?"

"What?"

"What a dump," she said.

"Okay, fine, don't tell me where you were."

"I was just outside, okay? Sorry if I don't feel completely comfortable treating you like my mommy and reporting to you about everywhere I've fucking been, okay?"

"Oh, is that you treating me like your mommy? Because I just thought that was being a courteous normal fucking person. I mean, you walk out of the fucking house in your underwear, of course I'm going to wonder, Oh, where is she?"

"I'm in my jammies, not my underwear."

She got a beer out of the fridge and drank it.

"Are you serious?" asked Randy.

"I guess that really depends on what you mean, doesn't it? Do you think it's a sign of a serious person to drink a beer at eight forty-five in the morning? Because I guess I think that makes it seem like I'm not really taking this very seriously."

"What do you mean, *this*?"

"You know," said Megan. She gestured vaguely to the apartment with her beer can.

"Oh my god, you're being so dramatic and corny right now I could shoot you," said Randy. Megan stood at the window with her back to him and finished the can of beer. "If someone else did this and I told you about it, you would make fun of that person."

Megan felt like her guts and bowels and all of that stuff were dangling over a pit. She needed someone to help her, obviously, but instead here she was, staring out of the window with her guts and anus dangling and swaying back and forth over a pit like a big pair of balls. Vulnerable as balls, too, and potent as balls, too, she thought, and then felt like a pretentious baby and started crying there in the glowing green spot near the window of her otherwise dank and dark and depressing apartment and she said "I hate you" in a way that would maybe be difficult to decipher, and since Randy was already fed up and practically over it, he didn't take the time to figure out what she'd said, which was ultimately maybe for the best.

"I'm going to take a shower," said Randy. "Help yourself to some coffee."

She turned and put her back against the window and, yeah, she definitely felt like an overdramatic idiot, but at least well, whatever. "Fucking asshole," she whispered. Fucking asshole.

She looked at herself in the bedroom mirror to determine whether or not a shower was necessary and decided it was not. She took off her jammies and used them to wipe the sweat from her asscrack and armpits, then she put on clean underpants and dug out her shorts which were, alas, too small, but would still button. She looked at that silly fuck in the mirror, did a royal bow, and said, "Fuck you, too."

She cleaned the apartment. It was a way to divert her nervous energy. She went on a walk. She waited for it to be night.

4

Jillian was either going to throw up or have diarrhea, her body hadn't decided which yet. It was nerves. Although, maybe nothing would happen. That was possible. She thought about it while she paced around her apartment. She had four T3s left, she could take them and then maybe they would help her calm down long enough (though they were the last, the very last) to come up with a plan.

"God, I wish I were hit by a deer," she said.

I would break my arms, Jesus, if I thought it would deliver me from this situation. Jesus, what can I do, what do you want me to do? You've kept me safe before and I trust that you will keep me safe now, or if you punish me, then it's for all the right reasons and things will be better after the punishment than they are now. But I also know you won't ever, you would not ever hurt a kid, and that's all I'm trying to do is to not hurt my kid and I would do anything, you know, I would really I would break my arms if you would just tell me how to get out of this.

Jillian dug her small fingers into the flesh of her arms and shuddered the word "fuck."

"Fuck," she said.

She resumed pacing. Her mouth became dry. After a few rounds of her apartment, she began to feel some kind of a release, which she interpreted as the beginnings of a divine intervention, but it was really an adrenaline crash and some dizziness from walking circles.

The golden hour came and Megan and Randy walked to the barbecue. A few times Megan punched Randy in the arm as hard as she could and Randy said, "Don't you fucking do that. Don't you fucking do that."

"Why are you such a fucking asshole all of a sudden?" she asked.

"I'm surprised you can't think of anything more interesting to say to me than that," he said.

"I guess my mind is too clouded with disgust."

"Oh, you're adorable," said Randy. "Hey, look, here we are. Hey, have fun tonight."

"You dick."

They walked to the backyard through a wooden gate. They walked down a gangway. Megan could hear it before she could see it. That stupid fucking tinkle or twinkle or whatever it is that a party has. That buzz, that hateful buzz. There were grills and Tiki Torches and street lamps back there, and as soon as they were spotted, Tiffany or Kimberly or whoever she was came over and hugged Randy and said how much she loved the website.

Great, thought Megan. I hate everyone here. She tried to find the beer, and it didn't take long. She drank in solitude, like some kind of disgusting shithead. "Doctor, how do you pronounce this l-e-p-r-o-s . . . s . . . y?" Three or four beers she drank just standing by the cooler alone. She tried to think about the movie *Sid & Nancy* and how cool it was, sometimes, to feel kind of nihilistic and self-destructive and a little "fuck the po-lice" but. "Alas," she whispered. "Alas, alas, alas." She lit a cigarette. She'd bought her own cigarettes so she wouldn't have to be beholden to Randy in any way tonight. She rehearsed announcing that she would be happy to sleep on the couch. A girl she sort of knew from school was looking at her from across the party. The girl walked over.

"I'll hang out with you for a while if you give me a cigarette," said the girl.

"Uh, sure," said Megan. "But the cigarettes are free to you, if that's what you prefer."

"No, I'll hang," said the girl. She must have been one of those "It's always good to have a new experience" people.

"I forgot your name," said Megan.

"It's Anthea," said the girl.

Anthea. Oh, right. Anthea.

"You see that guy?" asked Anthea.

"Yeah," said Megan.

"He can't see me smoking. He gets pissed when he sees me smoking. But he won't make a commitment to me, so fuck it, I can still smoke. If he made a commitment to me, I'd consider quitting."

"Well, you can use me to shield yourself from him if you want."

"I mean, I'm not a total asshole. I don't smoke in front of him, not even in my apartment. I never ask to smoke in his car. I'm considerate."

"Yeah. So, is he dating other people?"

"I don't know," said Anthea. "Probably, right?"

"That would seem usual." Megan sucked on her beer until it was gone, then opened another.

She remembered Anthea from classes they'd had together. Anthea was a few years younger than Megan and would say stuff like "You're so cool" but would bum cigarettes off of Megan and not really want Megan to say anything. She'd just stand there and talk about fights she was having with her friends and how some certain guy or whatever had slighted her, and Megan would interject awkwardly from time to time. But the awkward interjections didn't come from a real place of awkwardness, they were a sort of Kabuki awkwardness that amused Megan, so she usually welcomed this girl's company. Anthea was small and pretty in a weird way (which only made her prettier) and completely oblivious to body language and sarcasm. Either that or she was some kind of genius. Either oblivious or completely aware and playing a game.

Megan surveyed the yard, looking for Amanda.

Jillian was at home. She took the last four Tylenols and was singing along to the radio in the kitchen while Crispy and Adam watched TV in the living room. She danced a little, but not much.

Amanda was there, talking to Carrie. Whatever, thought Megan.

"It's, like, the opposite of the problem I had in high school, when I had three consecutive boyfriends and none of them would fuck me."

"Huh? Sorry, I missed the first part," said Megan.

"No, it's just that I'm sleeping with that guy over there and I'm also sleeping with another guy, but neither of them will date me. And I was just saying how that was, like, the opposite of my problem in high school. And it's just funny how your problems change all the time."

"Is that really the opposite problem?"

"Uh, yeah?"

"Hmm."

"What?"

"Well, I guess, in high school, having sex is a big commitment. It's something a girl can hold you to. Like, 'We had sex, you have to keep dating me!'"

"So, what are you saying?"

"I'm just saying your problem hasn't changed. It's the same problem. For some reason guys don't want to commit to you. It's probably in your personality or something."

Anthea made a face. "Ugh, what the fuck, you're right."

"Sorry," said Megan. "I shouldn't have said that."

"Hey, man, I don't give a fuck." Anthea shifted and drank her beer.

"I mean, it's like how I have this same problem of being an asshole to everyone all the time," said Megan.

"Oh, come on, you're not an asshole," said Anthea.

Megan wanted to say, "Who the fuck are you and what the fuck do you know about me? You have no idea who I am or what I think, so go fuck off." But then she would have to stand by herself.

Randy was still super pissed, and it was like every time he laughed or had a decent time, he was doing it to spite Megan, who he was pretty sure he was going to break up with sooner rather than later after today. God, just look at her over there. She already looked hammered and it was only nine.

Amanda kept shooting Megan glances and getting kind of mad that Megan wasn't coming over to say hello. Wouldn't that be the big thing to do? Every time they'd ever gotten into a fight, Amanda had been the person to make up, and she wanted proof this time that Megan could be the bigger person. It would be good for Megan to practice some humility. Unless the truth was that Megan didn't really want to be friends with Amanda, and in that case.

"Adam, honey, do you mind if Mommy goes to go and make a phone call?"

Adam shook his head.

Megan wondered if maybe she ought to go over and talk to Amanda and Carrie. What would happen if she walked over there and pretended like there was no beef between any of them? Would that be possible? That seemed to be everyone else's policy. Maybe she could try it.

Anthea was talking out her issues with Peter, the guy she was at the party with, and she was wondering if it was better to keep sleeping with him without them dating, or if she should offer him some kind of ultimatum and then (probably) get dumped and then wait around for someone who actually wanted to treat her decently. Learning a little self-respect might be a good thing. She wasn't so arrogant that she couldn't admit she didn't always have the most self-respect. She started nodding.

Jillian went into her bedroom and cradled her cell phone in her hands and looked at it and felt chilly because of the AC.

"What is your, like, ultimate goal? What would be the one wish you would ask to have granted right now, if you—I mean, if that could actually happen?"

Megan stumbled a little bit out of drunkenness and opened another beer. "I would like to have sex with an enormous man."

Anthea started laughing.

"No, I don't mean his penis or his height or anything, I mean enormous," she indicated this with her hands, spreading her arms wide and moving them in circular sorts of patterns, "to me. Enormous to me. I want to be psychically overwhelmed by a magical sex man."

Anthea started laughing.

"What about you?" asked Megan.

"I guess I want that, too."

"Hey, let's go talk to my friend Amanda over there."

"All right, I know her."

Randy watched Megan and the girl walk across the lawn toward Amanda and Carrie.

Adam was watching some show he didn't fully understand about the intelligence of dolphins. He knew he wanted to touch one, to ride one, to have a dolphin choose him as a companion. Then he would know for sure what he suspected to be true, that there was something particular about him. To be chosen by a dolphin would confirm that.

Crispy's skin felt brittle for some reason. Sort of staticky, electric. She rubbed her belly slightly on the carpet and chewed on the rawhide bone. The way it liquefied in her mouth was soothing. She was able to mark her progress by comparing the size of the bone to the size of her hands. It was good to have something to do, some kind of activity, even if you didn't really understand what you were doing or why you were doing it.

Amanda noticed, obviously, that Megan was walking up. Why was she with a friend? Who was this poor girl? Didn't this girl know what it was like to be friends with Megan, and just how fucking horrible that was? Was Megan going to apologize with witnesses around? Amanda prepared herself for anything.

"Hey," said Megan. "Do you guys know Anthea?"

Rats and squirrels frolicked in the alleys and yards respectively. Groups of raccoons walked around, crossing between alleys and streets, using the gangways. A drunk girl and her boyfriend were walking to the grocery store to get more alcohol, and the girl noticed two yellow-green disks and mistook them for dog's eyes, since they were attached to a head that was peeking out between the bars of a fenced-in yard. She thought the dog would be cute and she would say hi to it like she liked to do when she was drunk. As they got closer to the animal, she saw eight total of those yellow-green disks, realized they were raccoons, enormous raccoons, then screamed.

"Ah!"

"What?!" said her boyfriend. He put his arms around her. "What?"

She crouched down and started laughing hysterically. "Those fucking raccoons! I thought they were dogs, oh my god, they're so fucking creepy."

"Let's cross the street," said the boyfriend.

"Okay."

The raccoons watched the couple, perhaps understanding that they'd been laughed at. One of the raccoons belched softly.

The wind rustled the leaves, and the trees appreciated the feeling. A bird who was still awake sat on the branch of one of the trees and felt the warm breeze and listened to the sounds of the trees and the cars and smelled all of that freshness, and he inhaled, puffing up his cute little breast, and felt like he might cry, if only he could cry. If he could, he would, but out of an appreciation of beauty and inevitability, not out of sadness.

Carrie thought there was something sort of obnoxious about Megan. She'd heard about the fight between her and Amanda, obviously. She'd even heard about the part where Megan was crouched under the porch screaming and crying or whatever. But it was weird, here she was, acting sort of normal. Carrie examined her skeptically.

"Did you guys see the website?" asked Megan. "Randy did

it," she said, pointing to Randy with her thumb. "I think it looks pretty good."

And now it was easier because everyone was Anthea, and Megan was just riffing.

Elena was at home doing some needlepoint in front of the TV when her phone rang. She had the window open a crack and the fresh air filled her living room. Her boys were out, all of them (her husband, too), and she was working on a project that would be hung in the church. Everyone seemed to really like her needlepoint. This pattern was a line of interlocking flower branches surrounding a phrase about togetherness and sweetness and how the two were related and equal in the eyes of God. She was so happy about the way her life was sometimes. She had plenty to feel good about. She assumed the phone call would be her husband, and she felt so good she thought she would ask him to pick her up a treat from the store. Maybe a pie or ice cream, she wasn't sure what she wanted. She slipped the needle into her work, set it aside, and reached for the cordless.

"How's it going, Carrie?" Megan asked. She smiled. "How was your thirty-under-thirty interview?"

"It went pretty well. Everyone looks great in their photos. So, so pretty. I'm really excited to see the layout."

"You do design, right? Is that what you went to school for?" asked Megan. "For design?"

"Yeah, that and writing, painting, and photography."

"That's cool, like a mixed major. I bet that's really useful," said Megan.

"Hello," said Elena.

"Hello," said Jillian, but she said it in a hilarious, gruff Batman voice.

Megan's behavior made Amanda uncomfortable. Does she have a gun? Are we all about to die?

Jillian had a case of the giggles all night, and had to go into the bathroom twice just so Adam would stop asking her what was so funny. What was so funny was, for some reason, she'd decided to demand that Elena give her hundreds of dollars. Jillian believed in the power of Christ and she had promised earlier that she would trust in any idea He gave to her, and this was His idea. When she thought about it, she would laugh, then moan, then feel like she was going to puke, then feel nervous, then feel nothing. Then a few minutes later, the cycle would repeat. Similar to the feeling she'd had before she called Adam's dad. Like dread, but also inevitability.

"Yeah, it has been pretty useful," said Carrie.

"Do you have a preference between film and digital photography?" Megan asked.

"Well, I really love developing film and making prints in the darkroom. That was a lot of fun in school. But, for work, it's easier to use a digital camera. At first we used digital offset plates, which you just print out from a computer, rather than developing, and now we don't even use an offset printer. We just have a nice printer. If I used film, I'd have to print it, then scan it, then print it again, so . . . The pictures I get from a digital camera with a nice lens are great. And you can, of course, always manipulate the . . ."

Anthea was looking around, bored.

"Who is this? Can I help you?" asked Elena.

"This is Jillian," she said, still using the voice. "Jillian Bradley."

"Jillian, why are you talking like that?"

Jillian cleared her throat, opened her eyes and mouth as wide as she could, and then called on the power of God. "Sorry," she said in her normal voice.

It looked like Megan was smiling while she was talking to Carrie. Randy was watching her and felt nervous and noticed that Amanda looked nervous. But she probably just looked nervous because she and Megan hadn't made up yet. Probably.

"Jillian, what do you want?"

"It's not about what I want, it's about what I need. I know what you think of me. I'm not completely oblivious."

"I don't know what you're talking about," said Elena.

"Yes you do, okay? So let's just get that straight. I need you to give me eight hundred dollars for Adam's day care, and so that is what you are going to do. I need eight hundred dollars from you."

"Jillian, I'm not going to give you eight hundred dollars. That's absurd. If anything, you owe me one hundred dollars for all the gas I've been using getting your son off to day care, plus a little extra for my wasted time."

"You shriveled, heartless little bitch, you will give me eight hundred dollars or I will go through with it."

"Go through with what? You don't have the guts to do anything to me. You're weak and you're too much of an idiot to come up with a way to hurt me. Jesus, Jillian, what are you thinking?"

"Okay, I'm telling, then."

"Telling who?"

Jillian grinned and giggled, then whispered "God."

She continued to giggle and whisper things that were not words. She drew herself up into a ball.

Megan said a few things that made Carrie laugh and they were getting along fairly well.

"I think you're probably the most sick, ugly, hateful person in the entire world," said Jillian. "And so now I'm going to spend the rest of my energy letting God and Jesus know how much I hate you and how horrible you are and how much you deserve to suffer. You help me and you use it as a way to mock me? You do that and call yourself a Christian and think you won't suffer the eternal fire for the crime of blasphemy?"

"Jillian, this is absurd. I'm hanging up. I'm going to hang up," said Elena.

"I hope I die soon so I can tell God everything you've ever done to me," Jillian screamed.

Elena hung up the phone.

"Oh, god, you're so lucky, you know?" said Megan, leaning in toward Carrie and smiling.

"I guess so," said Carrie.

"I mean, you're just so lucky that you get to turn your passion and your art into something commercial. You know, something you can make money off of."

"Yeah, I love my job," said Carrie.

Megan's eyes flashed and she smiled wider. Amanda looked into that face and was frightened. She saw demons there. She saw through that smile and saw the poison in the eyes. Maybe it was the reflection of the Tiki Torches. Amanda drank from her beer and fumbled for a cigarette.

"It's just so nice to see an artist make money off of their passion. Kind of makes us all feel like it's not so hopeless after all," said Megan.

Did Megan's sentence trail off into a whisper, or was Amanda just transfixed by what she thought she saw in that expression?

"I have to go get another beer," said Anthea. Megan straightened up. She had been hunched toward Carrie and grinning.

"Yeah, I kind of have to piss," said Megan. She turned to smile at Amanda. The girls left. Carrie and Amanda looked confused.

Elena was standing, suddenly feeling creepy. She walked around her house to make sure all of her doors were locked. She put the safety stopper locks on the windows and called her husband to ask if he would come home. She went to the kitchen and leaned against the counter and put her hand to her mouth and shook. She did not shake for remorse, she shook for rage and fear for her personal safety. She imagined Jillian breaking into her house. Elena would decapitate her if she tried anything. She glanced at the knife drawer.

Megan tossed her empty into a trash can and walked up the back-porch steps. She had that kind of feeling that should probably be embarrassing, but is too overwhelming at the time to be embarrassing. That kind of studly, cinematic feeling that comes after a massive, psychic unburdening.

There was no one in the apartment. Megan pissed without turning on the light in the bathroom. When she was finished, she washed her hands with cold water because her fingers tended to get stiff and swollen in hot weather. She always wondered if that happened to everyone. She could hear the shrieks and chatter of the party outside. Someone started shooting bottle rockets.

Jillian hung up the phone and then lay down because she was already on her bed, so why not?

It was hard for Megan to make out what the living room looked like in the dark. The streetlights were visible through the open windows, and they had that hypnotic effect over Megan that bright things sometimes have over moths and the drunk. She walked to the windows. There were large plants in the living room and bookshelves and a television. A cat lay on the couch. If anyone came into the apartment she would say, "Oh, I'm just looking at the cat." People love to look at cats.

She put her palms on the windowsill and looked out onto the street. Even though it was cooler now, a bead of sweat ran down her asscrack. A cyclist rode past and a guy stumbled around on the pavement. Megan zoned out. Megan turned to the cat.

"I envy you, you fucking idiot," she said to it telepathically.

It squirmed and said, "Whatever."

She sighed. She looked out the window and again thought about taking some kind of long road trip or maybe faking a fugue state or maybe drinking so much or becoming so stressed out that she actually entered a fugue state. When she came to, she would work on getting it together. Et cetera.

There were very few cars out on the street. Everyone must be drinking, she thought.

It was difficult for Jillian to sit up and, when she did, she felt like a ghost, like she was sending her avatar to continue her life while she was really still there on the bed. This feeling had happened before. It was fun in a certain way, because of how she felt like she was floating around, which made her feel, even if she didn't think it specifically, as if there were some kind of random current to life sloshing her toward her fate.

She sat next to Adam on the couch. They didn't speak. They watched the program about the sentient dolphins.

Megan and Randy walked home together. Megan started crying and Randy held her hand. They fought again in the morning. Sunday was a generally bad day. Megan smoked a lot and sat outside on the curb and fantasized about fugue states.

Jillian took the battery out of her phone and hid it somewhere in her house, then sat down and consciously forgot where she put it. Then, since it was Sunday, she observed that it was her day of rest.

5

Things kept happening the way they would. On Monday it was still warm. Megan took a shower and shaved her legs, bikini area, and armpits, put on lotion and deodorant, then put on a decent outfit. She got on the bus and sat in a patch of sun and put a book in her lap, but wasn't able to read it. She was spaced out. A really loud guy got on the bus.

"Ugh, I lost my cell phone," he shouted. Megan watched him. The guy looked around and noticed another guy, similarly dressed, look up at him. "Hey, man, can I use your cell phone?" he asked.

The similarly dressed guy said "Sure" kind of quietly and handed his phone to the loud guy.

"Hey, man, this is Jim. Yeah, I'm on the bus right now. Yeah, I'm at North and Halsted. Yeah, so I guess I'm gonna be there in like twenty minutes, okay? Okay. Okay," said the loud guy. He hung up and gave the phone back. "Thanks, man," he said. "I'm an event promoter." The other guy nodded. "And I lost my cell phone, so it's like, man, I'm drowning over here without my phone, you know?"

"Oh, yeah, I know how that is."

"Yeah, you know. And it's not the value of the phone that I'm worried about. I don't care about the value of the phone, it's the value of all of those contacts."

"Oh yeah," said the other guy.

"I'm on my way up to go get my cell phone right now. The lady who found it called around to get in touch with me. I feel lucky about that."

"Oh, yeah. You know there's still good people in the world."

"That is right. You know, I was working all weekend at those two Temptations shows. You like The Temptations?"

"Oh, yeah, Big Daddy Williams."

"Oh, yeah! So I was dancing with my girl, taking a break from working, and my phone slipped out of my pocket. And it was, like, the end of it for me. I thought I was going to lose my position. Because I'm my own boss. But I can't do my work without those contacts."

The other guy nodded. The loud guy continued.

"But then this lady called my girl up and said she had my phone. And now here you are, lending me your cell phone. And that's just so great of you, man. I mean, I might have lost everything if you hadn't lent me your phone, I'm serious."

"Well, I believe that good deeds are returned. And I believe that we're all in the right place at the right time to help each other out or to not help each other out, depending on the way we feel moved to act. It's an invisible impulse, but I think, and I don't know if this is too much to say, but I think it's something else that's telling us how to act."

"That's a deep feeling, friend," said the loud guy.

The two guys continued to talk about the invisible accidents of politeness and cruelty or whatever and, eventually, Megan tuned them out and turned to the window.

Ring 12/10/20